IT ISN'T CHEATING
IF HE'S DEAD

JULIE FRAYN

5

Publications

ISBN 978-0-9918510-3-4

Dedication

For Brynn and Charlie. Everything is for you. Because of you. I love you both.

Acknowledgements

I have the world's greatest children. I know what you're thinking - everyone thinks their children are the best. Honestly, I am not biased, simply observant. My kids rock, and I'd be nothing without their love, humour, sarcasm, hugs, and kisses. Thank you Brynn and Charlie. For making me proud every day, and for being proud of me.

I am indebted to my beta readers: Brynn Archibald, Carolyn Frayn, Deb Grondin-White, Barb Munro, Sandra Kam, Laren Murphy, Alida Visbach, Jo Morris, Joanne Dutka, Jen Chatfield, Shelley Priebe, and Michelle Wesley-Schmidt.

Last, but definitely far from least, I would be nowhere without my wonderful editor, Scott Morgan (www.write-hook.com). I highly recommend him. What are you waiting for? Go hire him!

more like the accursed

Not every knock brings opportunity. Not the promise of something wonderful. Sometimes you have to open the door anyway, so another can be allowed to close.

Jemima Stone balanced her cell phone between her shoulder and her ear. The accordion file she couldn't cram into her overloaded briefcase was squished under her arm, her elbow squeezed against it while she fumbled the key into the lock. The deadbolt resisted and she gave the brass knob a hard twist until the door popped open.

"Yes, Richard. I know you're innocent." That's what they all said. She pressed the toe of her sensible black pump against the door and pushed it shut. It bounced against the warped jamb.

"We've got a decent case. But I'm not sure how to get around the fact that your brother is testifying for the prosecution." She shouldered the door closed. Her cell phone slipped against her sweaty cheek, the accordion file slid back, spurted out from under her arm and hit the hardwood. The worn cardboard broke open and spewed paper all over the entryway.

"Damn it." The phone fell. She let her tattered, years-old briefcase slam into the oak, and snatched the new smart phone before it cracked open against the floor like her last one. "No, no. Not you Richard. Sorry." She ran her free hand through her hair. "I want you to be absolutely certain of this innocent plea. That video he

1

has of you huddled over your mother's jewelry box is pretty compelling." She kicked off her shoes, aimed for the mat inside the door. Missed again.

She rolled her eyes and tapped one bare foot. When would she find an actual innocent client to defend?

"Yeah, yeah, I know. Expectation of privacy. Not sure it applies when you sneak into someone else's home." She started up the stairs, unzipped her skirt and unhitched her bra along the way. "Yes Richard, I believe you."

Like hell she did.

"I'll try to get it excluded. Talk to you later."

She stepped into the bedroom, ended the call and tossed the phone on the night stand. Her grey pencil skirt fell to the floor. She stepped out of it and left it where it landed. She tossed her old black suit jacket and outdated, pink paisley blouse with the hole in one armpit towards the small chair in the corner. Her aim as true as ever, they landed on the carpet. Her support bra and black lace thong followed right behind. She flopped face first into her billowy comforter and groaned, then rolled onto her back.

Defending the wrongfully accused in real life was nothing like in books and movies. Where was Atticus Finch when you needed him? It would help if her clients were all innocent like they claimed to be. She had to believe them. Or at least say she did.

The clock radio glowed ten-fifteen. Another fourteen-hour day slogging through evidence and interviewing witnesses, trying to find the oomph to defend the indefensible.

Her cell phone rang. She snatched it from the night stand and eyed the screen. "Shit, really?" Did they all think she lived and breathed their cases? Their lives? What about her own life? Screw it. She pushed the 'ignore' button. Edward wasn't going anywhere, stuck in the remand centre, waiting for sentencing. Too late, buddy.

The judge saw through your lies and found you as guilty as you are. Filing an appeal could wait until morning.

Where the hell did her passion go? That drive and compulsion to prove the prosecutors wrong, get her clients cleared at all costs? All legal costs. Swirling the drain with her clients' morals and ethics, that's where. They were more like the accursed than the accused.

She ran the tap until steam poured out from behind the shower curtain, then stepped under the pounding water. With every scrub of loofah against her soft, pale skin and every rinse-and-repeat of sweet, flowery, herbal shampoo lather in her auburn hair, the guilty and the liars washed away. For today. It'd be same old, same old come morning. How could she be jaded and aching to retire at the ripe old age of thirty-one? She'd never make partner at this rate. Did she even want that anymore? Nothing in her life had made sense since four years ago this coming June twelfth.

Jemima pulled on the yoga pants and tank top that lay across the end of her bed where she'd discarded them when she got dressed that morning.

Gerald's small mahogany chest sat on the right side of their dresser. She hadn't opened it in two years. Hadn't even moved it. Just tidied around it when she tidied at all.

With the tip of her index finger she wiped a thick layer of dust from the small latch. She stared at the chest and scraped her top teeth over her bottom lip. She lifted the latch and opened the lid. The ring she'd given him to commemorate their engagement sat on top of a pile of coins. Business cards were strewn about the burgundy velvet-lined interior. A lone bottle of clozapine lay tipped on its side, the little green antipsychotic pills long since expired. He'd left behind all the things that had worked so hard to keep him sane.

She knocked the lid closed, flinched at the crack of wood on wood so loud in the quiet house. The very quiet house. She'd known he was off his meds. But why didn't he take his damn ring?

She pulled the drapes and stared westward. There were no mountains in the dark. No purple silhouettes, no white capped spring peaks. She lived spitting distance from the most beautiful mountain region on earth, but she rarely bothered to leave Calgary, satisfied to just soak it all in from afar. She made a mental note to look out the window in the morning. And maybe take a drive out to Banff next weekend.

A quiet rap at the front door shook the leaded glass in its frame. She glanced at the clock. Ten forty-five. Who on earth would be coming by at that hour?

At the entry, she drew back the white lace curtain from the small window that overlooked her front porch. It wasn't necessary. The curtain was sheer. She'd recognized the trim and solid form of Detective Wight halfway down the stairs, the angle of his square jaw, a mirror reflection of his jar-head haircut. He was all slants and corners and points and sharpness, his voice crisp and tight and all business. Oh what ripped muscles must live inside that well-pressed suit?

A spasm grew in her stomach. He never showed up this late. His regular updates were Saturday afternoons or early evenings. Was today the day?

She smoothed the front of her pants with both palms and shook her hands in a vain attempt to ease the tension from her arms. She twisted her head side to side and released a loud crack from the base of her neck. She sighed and reached for the doorknob.

The brass was cold in her hand and took extra effort to turn. When the tumbler released the latch and the wood of the eighty-year-old door popped open, the hinges creaked.

She really should get that fixed.

"Hello, Detective." She didn't open the screen. Didn't offer to let him in. Her heart weighed a hundred pounds.

"Hi, Jem. It's Finn, please?"

He was soft spoken tonight. Even his face yielded its rigidity, his eyes soft, like his sculptor had smoothed out the rough edges of his clay.

"Can I come in?"

"Yeah. Sorry, Finn."

He pulled the screen wide to give room for his broad shoulders to pass, and stepped across the threshold.

She crossed her arms. "You found him. Right? That's why the late visit? The quiet voice?"

All the softened edges.

"I'm sorry, Jem."

She shuffled to the kitchen table and fell into a chair. An old pack of cigarettes that sat untouched on the sideboard appeared in her hand. She pulled one out. There wasn't a lighter in the house. Not even a match. She hadn't smoked in seven months. She brought the cigarette up in front of her eyes and sniffed it. She set her jaw and flicked the cigarette onto the table. It bounced and rolled off the edge.

Finn pulled out the chair opposite her. Its wooden legs creaked under his six-three-plus frame. He leaned over and plucked the cigarette from the floor and returned it to the pack.

She fought back tears. "What happened to him?"

"We're not sure of everything yet. Lots of pieces to put together."

"Where was he?"

"They found him —" He took a deep breath and seemed to hold it far too long before letting it go. "Shit, Jem. He was in a dumpster in an alley. In Montreal."

She clenched her eyes shut. Tears won the battle and squeezed out from all sides. "How?"

"He'd been beaten. Shot. Probably robbed. He had nothing on him, no wallet, no money, no jacket. Not even shoes."

She opened her eyes. Finn was misty too. Almost four years had passed since Gerald went missing. With all the updates from Detective Wight, the phone calls, the meetings, there'd been no sign of chinks in his cop armor. It was good to know he had some. Good to know he was human.

"Who killed him? Why? How did he get to the other side of the country? And where the hell has he been for four damn years?"

"All questions I can't answer today. The Montreal police are working on it. It's a murder case now, in their territory." He reached across the table and covered her trembling hand with his big paw. "Jem. I'm going to find out everything. I promise."

"Yeah. Sure."

"We know where he started. We know where he ended up. We've got some clues to fill the gap, like when you saw him downtown that time. We'll figure it out."

"I have to call his mother. And his research partner. And. And." She pulled her hand away and chewed on her thumbnail. "And a bunch of other people I don't want to talk to."

"I'll get out of your way." He stood and turned towards the door.

"Wait." She pushed herself to her feet, balanced on her tiptoes, threw her arms around his neck and placed a light kiss on his cheek. "Thank you. For everything."

He gave her a gentle squeeze. When she relaxed her hug he held on for an obvious second before letting her go. "I'll keep in touch. We'll keep up the weekly reports too. This won't go cold."

"I appreciate that."

She walked him to the entryway and watched him descend the

crumbling concrete steps to his unmarked car parked on the street. The faint scent of cologne sweetened the still air. The detective was a big man, but she could see no sign of flab. It was obvious from how his clothes hung that he was muscular, but that hug proved he was solid. He must scare the shit out of the bad guys.

His car pulled out from the curb and turned up the street. She put her shoulder to the door and forced it into the jamb.

She passed the table and snapped up the cigarette pack on the way by. She tapped it once against the heel of her palm and a cigarette slid out. She lit a burner on the gas stove. Seven months smoke-free. She'd sworn it was the last time she would quit. Even started exercising to combat the weight gain. Fat lot of good it did her. Fifteen pounds on and then off again with each win and eventual loss against the addiction.

Screw it.

She held the tip to the blue flame and sucked in a long drag. Her lungs filled with glorious poison, nerves relieved and senses heightened all at once. She let the smoke slip from her lips and pass in front of her eyes, then tilted her head back and blew the rest straight up to the ceiling.

The stench of stale cigarette smoke had finally been cleansed from her home, from the drapes and the upholstery. Gerald would've made her take it outside. She glanced at the back door and the chilly, black night. She pulled a tumbler out of the cupboard and filled it with merlot from the open bottle that sat at the ready on the faux-granite countertop, then dragged herself into the living room.

The under-stuffed sofa that Gerald had picked out the year they moved in together accepted her into its rigid discomfort. Her forearm landed in its usual spot on the balding armrest. She placed the tumbler on the coffee table next to a stack of dusty coasters and sucked on her cigarette until the long ash fell into her lap. She flicked the ash onto the area rug and wiped it in with her feet. The wine went down in one long gulp. She pitched the smoldering butt into the glass, its heat hissing in the skiff of red liquid that remained. She tucked her legs beneath her, dropped her forehead to her forearms, and sobs overtook her.

Four years. Searching. Hoping. Wondering. Anticipating. And for nothing. Gerald was gone. More often than not she'd thought they wouldn't find him alive. How could they? But she held onto any shred of optimism she could find. If he'd stayed on his meds maybe he could have gotten his schizophrenia under control. Or at least been able to manage it. Stay with her. Marry her. Keep his promises.

But he didn't. He couldn't. What other outcome could there have been?

She crossed the room to the bookshelf next to the television and picked up a pewter frame. In the picture, Gerald shook the hand of the dean of medicine, accepting an award for excellence in cancer research. Gerald. Mussed-up sandy hair resting on his shoulders. Ebony eyes. Jeans and a black tee under that damn lilac corduroy sport coat. Those silly boat shoes.

How ironic that he published papers on the dichotomy between theory and practice. He was a walking dichotomy. A living, breathing contradiction. Or at least he used to be.

When he started hearing voices, letting "the others" dictate the direction of his research, change the direction of his theory, it all went to shit. He was diagnosed with schizophrenia a year after it started. And the year after that he was gone. His mind, his life, his work. Him. All gone.

She put the frame down and glanced at the wall. The hole he'd made when he ripped the old television cable out stared at her like a one-eyed monster. She'd fixed the cable not long after Gerald disappeared but had never gotten around to patching the hole. A reminder of one of the scarier moments. When the characters on the screen started watching him. Whispering about him. When he'd had enough of their interference and their spying and he killed them all with one angry yank of the cord. The television lay dormant those last two weeks. No radio was allowed either. And the phone, well that was off limits in his presence. The real world was watching. The make believe world was watching.

No one was watching.

six bottles of grief

Jem stared at the hairline cracks in the ceiling and ignored the radio alarm that blared one classic rock tune after another. She slapped the snooze button for the fifth time. The side of her hand clipped the tumbler on the night stand, jostling the inch of merlot left behind. Five-thirty-six.

Damn it.

How do you measure grief? Two sleepless nights. Six bottles of wine. Four three-hour-long baths. Two tubs of butterscotch ripple ice cream. Zero phone calls made. Zero visits to the park. Zero sandwiches delivered. Zero trips to the grocery store. One unanswered knock at the door.

She couldn't even face Finn. Couldn't face anyone.

Gerald's funeral had to wait. The medical examiner wouldn't release him yet. Evidence could still be gleaned from the wounds on her fiancé's dead body, in the folds of his decomposing flesh, from the long strands of his once beautiful hair.

Was it still long when he died? He wasn't recognizable enough for anyone to identify his body. Dental records proved it was him. She didn't have to face him. Didn't have to remember him dead and mutilated. It was hard enough to shake the imaginary pictures she made up in her head. How could she have ever gotten past the real thing?

His warm smile, warm body, his patchouli-meets-Old Spice scent, his dedication and drive and intelligence. That was the Gerald she would remember. The way he was in the pictures. Before the crazy came.

Even if they did release his body, she couldn't plan the funeral. She hadn't even called his mother. And it wasn't going to happen today. No way could she face that woman yet, even if only on the phone. What was the rush? Gerald wasn't going anywhere.

She swung her legs over the side of the bed. Her feet landed on a pile of clothes. She shoved them aside with her toes and sighed, then gathered them up and dropped them into a laundry basket already spilling over with bed sheets. She kicked all the used wet towels out of the bathroom, through the door, and down the stairs to the hardwood entry below.

The linen closet gave up its last clean towel. She lingered in the shower, letting the hot water tank drain and the water run cold against her skin. After towel-drying her hair, she threw on her morning clothes — denim capris, a black tank over her most comfortable, most ugly, most full-support bra. She slid the bedroom drapes open. The Rocky Mountains jutted from the horizon, the rising sun illuminating their snow-capped peaks. Not a cloud in the western sky. She pulled a light sweater from her closet.

The aroma of fresh coffee met her halfway down the stairs. Her heart sank. How many mornings would she greet before the expectation that he'd be in the kitchen waiting for her would pass? Gerald had bought that fancy machine. She still made coffee every night before bed and set it to brew for the same time she still set her alarm to wake her. The same time that Gerald had always awoken. Same old, same old. But the daily practice of leaning on the counter across from each other, discussing their plans for each day, his research, her cases, well — that ended weeks before he disappeared.

11

Damn, how she hated the others. Had grown so tired of Gerald telling her their thoughts. She didn't give a rat's ass if they said banana peels and coconut oil was the new cure for cancer. All that mattered to her was what Gerald thought. But he didn't know anything by then, didn't have opinions of his own. He only cared about the others. And what they told him to do.

The signs were there long before she did something about it. She'd beaten herself up over that for all these years. His devolution from brilliant to quirky to confounding to bat-shit nuts took a mere few months. When he refused to take his medication, a psychotic break wasn't far behind. Then he was just gone.

She'd given up any semblance of a personal life since. Her world became cases and clients and coping. Muddling through each day wondering where he was, why he left. If he was ever coming home.

After a year without him, her legal assistant, Cecilia, tried to fix her up on a blind date. She couldn't do it. Wouldn't do it. Gerald was only missing. And she still loved him, despite the fact he'd lost his mind. How could she cheat on him? Forget about him? Move on with her life? And how the hell was she going do that now? Now that she had no choice.

She pulled open the door to the basement and shoveled laundry down the steps with the side of one foot. Towels landed on the concrete and she slid the basket behind them. It caught on one wooden riser midway and toppled down the stairs, strewing underwear and yoga pants and tank tops in its wake.

"Shit." She stared at the mess for a few seconds then slammed the door closed with a flick of her wrist.

While two sugars dissolved in a travel mug of black coffee she plucked empty wine bottles that littered the kitchen off the counter and tucked them in a box under the sink for recycling. She shoved an empty ice cream carton in the garbage, wiped the counter clean with a wet paper towel and yanked open the fridge.

She pulled lunch meat from the refrigerator, peeled the cellophane from a pack of pastrami, sniffed and recoiled. Damn. She pitched it into the garbage and dug an unopened container from the back of the meat drawer. Still good for another week. Smoked turkey and black forest ham were salvaged, but three other opened packs of green-tinged processed lunch meat were tossed into the bin. Thank goodness for canned tuna. It never went bad.

She slapped mustard on rye bread to hold the meat in place, mixed tuna with mayonnaise, bits of green onion and diced pickles, and spread it between slices of whole wheat. She wrapped each sandwich in parchment paper. She used to use plastic baggies, but too many of them ended up in the bushes instead of the garbage cans that dotted the park. At least parchment was biodegradable.

She slid the knives and cutting board into the sink already brimming with dirty dishes. Time to get it together Jemima. Life does go on.

An hour later, she piled a heavy box of sandwiches and oranges and a flat of juice boxes into her van.

The sun was low on the horizon but sparkling bright in a cloudless sky. It promised to be another warm April day. A perfect day. Weather-wise. The rest of it could bite her well-rounded ass.

A cool breeze, ripe with wet grass, dirty snow, and mushy dog shit — the perfume of springtime in the Rockies — swirled around her and blew hair into her face. She brushed it from her eyes and tucked it behind her ears.

The neighbourhood was still quiet at this hour. Every neighbour was retired and pushing seventy, eighty, or more. She'd grown accustomed to being the young one on the block. Why Gerald thought this was the perfect place to raise kids was beyond her. It triggered one of their pre-psychotic arguments. She lost. She usually did. But in the end, he was right. A young neighbourhood full of screaming brats would have driven her to join him on the crazy train.

The engine turned over and she let it idle while she sipped strong coffee and fingered the pack of cigarettes she'd tucked into her pocket. She tossed it on the dash, pulled away from the curb and turned towards downtown.

The drive was easy. The early risers made their way along the city streets, content to get up at the crack of dawn to avoid rush hour traffic and guarantee a daily spot to park. A challenging task after eight.

The mountains glowed purple and orange in the distance. One of the beauties of living in this city, they could be seen from almost anywhere. The wilderness and craggy terrain not so close that her ears popped just driving a few miles, but not so far that families of deer surprised her on the front lawn a few times each year. And the rabbits. So many jackrabbits. She always let them nest in her yard. Over the years they learned to trust her enough to perk up and be ready to bolt, but not race away when she walked past.

She pulled up along the river drive and parked in her usual spot. She loaded a twonie into the meter, pulled the wagon from the rear of the van, and piled the food and drinks onto the wagon. She pushed her sunglasses onto her head, rubbed sweat from the bridge of her nose, then tapped them back to her face with one finger. The van honked to announce it was securely locked. She dropped the keys in her sweater pocket and picked up the wagon handle. The rubber wheels against the cracks in the sidewalk announced her approach before she saw any movement.

"Ruby! Where ya been?" Angus stood and stretched, leaving his favourite summer sleeping spot under the elm at the river's edge. He nudged his best friend with the toe of his worn boot. "Get up, Frankie. Ruby's here. We got breakfast."

She hadn't missed two days of deliveries in more than a year, and only then when she was ill with the flu.

"Morning, Angus." The smell of him always found her before he got anywhere near. She'd grown accustomed to the stench. Hadn't flinched at it in more than a year.

Angus called her Ruby since the first day she showed up in the park two years before. A conversation they had a week after they met ran through her mind.

"If you call me Jem, maybe I can spot you two juice boxes."

"Ruby. Gem. Same thing, no?" His laughter, like his throat was full of gravel, filled the quiet street.

"Different kind of Jem, mister."

He never did quit calling her Ruby. And now it was her favourite nickname.

Frank came up behind Angus and tossed an arm over his buddy's shoulder. "We missed you, angel. Why'd you forsake us the past two days, huh? Find some more handsome guys to hang around with?" He threw her an exaggerated wink and the two friends slapped each other on the back and laughed until they coughed.

"No more handsome dudes than you, I'm afraid." She handed them each a sandwich, an orange, and a juice box. "It's pretty quiet this morning. Where is everybody?"

Angus scratched his head and glanced around the park. "Shelter had stew last night. Maybe they stayed."

"And there's the new guy scaring everybody away. He's a damn freak." Frank poked his thumb across the park. "But like hell am I giving up my spot for that stinking shelter. Not to some skinny-ass Johnny-come-lately."

Fifty yards away, a bundle of brown canvas jacket and torn blue jeans sat at attention. His body was tucked halfway into the branches of a tall shrub. His khaki cap was pulled down, shading most of his face. His stare pierced right through her.

"When did he show up?"

"Day before yesterday, hey Frankie? He wandered around the corner, sat there and hasn't moved since. I don't even think he's taken a whiz."

"Well, I've got lots of sandwiches. You boys want a couple more? I'll see if your new friend wants some, then drop the rest at the shelter."

"You're a sweetheart, Ruby, love of my life." Angus took two ham sandwiches and shoved them in the inside pocket of his trench coat. "Speaking of which, any word on your missing man?"

She turned away and gazed towards the river. "Yeah. They found him."

"That's wonderful news, love."

"No, Frank. It's not. He's dead."

Angus and Frank stared at her in silence. Frank reached up and patted her shoulder three robotic times. "I. I'm sorry, Jem."

"Yeah, me too Ruby."

"Thanks. It shouldn't be such a shock, really. He's been gone so long. I'd often thought that he might be dead. But I always hoped he'd come home." She took hold of the wagon handle before grief overtook her. She shined a bright, fake smile on them. "Well, I'll see you tomorrow. Let me see if I can break in the new guy for you."

She made her way around the park and chatted with the regular residents. Each encounter brought her nearer to the new guy. When the last resident was fed, she glanced towards the shrub.

His eyes glinted hate and anger from under the brim of his cap. Matted ash-blonde hair hung past his shoulders. He stared at her as she neared, his gaze intense, his posture stiff.

Her heart hammered and a bead of sweat broke out on her upper lip. She'd never been nervous in the park before. She considered passing him by. But his sunken cheeks and bony fingers broke her heart.

"Hello. I'm Jem. Would you like something to eat?"

He stared, didn't move a hair, didn't blink. She bent over the wagon and chose pastrami — the fat would do him good. When she straightened up, his eyes darted from the food to her face.

So he wasn't a statue.

"Here you are. I have ham if you'd prefer."

Nothing. Not one twitch. Just uncomfortable scrutiny from blazing grey eyes. His skin was tanned and weathered from exposure, but he was young. Not much older than Jem. He had a watchful intelligence about him. He looked sober, not strung out. He didn't even look nuts. And she knew from nuts.

"How about I leave it for you? If you don't want it, someone else will take it." She took two hesitant steps forward and placed the sandwich on the dirt in front of him.

His gaze moved to the food and then back to her face. No movement of the head, only the shifting of his eyes. Maybe he couldn't attack her if he wanted to. But he couldn't be paralyzed, he got himself there. He sat straight as an arrow, like a military man. Or a cop.

"What's your name?"

Nothing.

"I come by every morning. If you like turkey or tuna better, let me know. I can make anything you want."

Nothing.

"Okay then. Here's some juice and an orange." She placed them beside the sandwich. His eyes tracked her movements. "I'll see you tomorrow."

She pulled the wagon down the sidewalk, resisting the urge to look over her shoulder. At the corner she pushed the button to cross.

When the walk light lit, she glanced back. Angus and Frank sat at the far end of the short park, chewing with their mouths open and patting each other on the shoulder. She grinned and shook her head. They spent time reliving their glory day tales, one-upping each other's stories but never losing their camaraderie. It passed the time. That, and searching for food, begging for cash and booze, and bumming cigarettes off anyone that wandered by.

How many times had they told her about high stakes business deals gone wrong? How they'd met at the peak of their careers, and tumbled from the top of the mergers-and-acquisitions ladder to land in a heap of shit at the bottom. They claim to be happier now. No stress. No boss. No problem. It was hard to believe any of it was true.

She snuck one last peek at the new guy. The food sat untouched at his feet.

hip hop sex

"Hi, Mother Wolfe." Jem twisted a lock of hair around her index finger until it throbbed and turned purple. "I've got news."

Silence in Vancouver. Then the rasping breath of Gerald's dying mother. "So? Out with it already. He's not come home or you would have said so right off."

"No, he's not home. He won't ever be coming home."

"I see."

Four years of assuming the worst prepares you for just that. Jem knew that first hand.

A wheezy sigh crackled across the line. "When is the funeral?"

"I don't know. They're holding his body for evidence."

"Evidence? Of what? Wasn't it suicide?"

"Suicide? Of course not. Althea, he was murdered."

"B-but why? Who? Oh my God, no." Althea's voice cracked and gave way to soft sobs followed by hacking phlegmy coughs.

Jem winced and pulled the phone from her ear until the coughing stopped. "That's why they're keeping him. They don't know the answers yet." She pushed her palm against a spasm growing in her abdomen. "Did he know anyone in Montreal?"

"I don't think so. Is that where he's been?"

"Yes. For the last several months anyway. I'm trying to help the detective fill in some blanks, but I'm afraid I don't know as much as I thought."

"Well, clearly I don't either. You make sure they don't give up on him, you hear me?"

"I will."

"And you tell me what's going on. Don't just ignore me like you've been doing."

Jem grit her teeth. "I wasn't ignoring you, Althea." She was simply avoiding the bitch. "I just had nothing to tell you until now. I'll let you know what I find out, if I find anything out." She took a deep breath. No fighting with this woman, not today. "When it's time, do you want me to send him home to you? We can have the funeral there."

A quiet pause deadened the air between them. "Thank you. Yes. I would appreciate that."

Gerald was convinced his research would cure his mother. She'd developed small tumors on her ovaries when he was ten. The treatments of the day robbed her of her hair and her dignity. She was stripped of estrogen, forced into early menopause, eliminating the possibility of siblings for Gerald. Not that her age hadn't already taken that possibility off the table, but she loved to regale anyone who would listen with her sad tale of being forced to have only one child.

Althea never fully recovered. Each new diagnosis, each tiny slow tendril of disease that sucked vitality from her pushed him toward his career in cancer research. The fact that she continued to breathe all these years later was a medical miracle. And she gave him full credit for that, even though it was the tireless attention of the oncologists and a medical team of experts that kept her alive.

No wonder she didn't trust Jem with his heart. Or anyone else for that matter.

Althea's health was the topic of countless discussions between

Jem and Gerald, dozens of disagreements, and more than one near-brawl. There wasn't a hope in hell Mrs. Wolfe would live long enough for his research to pan out, let alone outlive her son. His research needed to be more focused, more specialized. Ovarian cancer, where it all began. Or breast or cervical. Hell, even pancreatic or testicular. It was too late to save his mother, Jem had argued, but if he put his brilliance toward something more specific, maybe he could save a million others. He never agreed, never listened. He kept on the path of studying all cancer, trying for the global magic cure pill that would put his mother right. Maybe he would have done it. What the hell did she know about it anyway? She was a lawyer, not a scientist.

When the others started telling him his mother would die, he believed them. But it didn't spur him to focus his research. He gave up on it altogether. Gave up on his mother. Gave up on himself. And gave up on Jem too.

"I'm so sorry, Althea. I loved your son. You do know that?"

"I'm sure you did the best you could. He claimed to love you. I never understood it. Why he didn't fall for one of the slender church-going beauties I set him up with I'll never understand. They would have had my grandchildren, stayed home. Taken proper care of my son."

Here we go again.

Jem grit her teeth. "You know that we planned on having a family. But he disappeared before we could."

"And you would have kept your precious career, let some nanny raise that child." Althea drew a deep wheezing breath. "No wonder he left you."

"He was a paranoid schizophrenic, Althea. He didn't wake up one day and decide to go. He was sick. It had nothing to do with me." Or so she kept telling herself.

21

"So they say. I have my doubts. Anyway, what does it matter now?"

Jem cleared her throat. "Right. Okay then. I'll be in touch." She pressed the end button and chucked the handset onto the table. It slid across the surface and crashed to the floor on the other side.

Jem shook her head. "Fuck." She grabbed a cold beer from the fridge and headed upstairs, her feet filled with cement.

She scanned the bedroom. All this time and his things were right where he left them, only disturbed long enough to dust around them when she bothered to dust at all. Daily drudgery loses importance, has no real value, when faced with daily dread.

She sat on the floor and opened the bottom drawer of the highboy where Gerald kept his pants. Each pair remained folded, stacked, and at the ready. She pulled them out and made three short piles of denim and canvas and corduroy. Throw away pile for anything holey or stained. Only one of those — his painting pants. Donation pile for the shelter and some of her sandwich buddies. And a keep pile. Because she loved the smell of him on the fabric. Because stroking the nap of the corduroy made him alive in the room. Because she wasn't ready to let go. Not yet.

She sighed and rested a hand on the keep pile — the tallest. Come on Jemima, exactly what critical memory did worn khaki cargo pants and faded dungarees hold? All of the keep pile was shoved next to the donations. Time to get real.

She took a long pull on the beer and set the sweaty green bottle on the hardwood. The potential for a water stain crossed her mind. That would have driven Gerald nuts.

She smirked. Yeah, that's what sent him over the edge. Not enough coasters.

The first thing she pulled from the second drawer was his favourite sweater. She closed her eyes and buried her face in the itchy grey wool. A hint of patchouli still survived in the loose knit, mingled with four-year-old body odour. She lay back on the floor and hugged it into her chest. Tears dripped from her temples onto the oak.

He wore that sweater often, but it was the day they moved into the house that always came to mind. She was still harbouring some bitterness that he'd won the fight to live in this antique neighbourhood, under this decades old leaky roof. Silence was her game while they unloaded boxes from the rented van that fall Saturday afternoon and shuffled past each other at the threshold. The chill in the air swept into their new living room through the open door. Or maybe the chill came from the tension between them.

Gerald grabbed the last box and headed inside while she locked up the van. She stepped into the house and shouldered the door shut, clicking the brass deadbolt into place.

In the living room he had set their small stereo on a box of books and attached his iPod. He stood with his back to her. The thumping sound of hip hop music jolted from the speakers, bounced off the walls, and shook the window pane. Then he pumped his hips three times and jumped, turned mid air, and landed facing her.

He lip-synced the words and danced like a fool, pretending to hold a microphone to his mouth. At the chorus, he sang out loud.

"It's getting hot in here." He pulled his grey wool sweater over his head, the white t-shirt he wore underneath bunching under his armpits. "So hot." He swung the sweater above his head. "So take off all your clothes." He let the sweater go and it flew across the room, hitting her square in the face. "I am, getting so hot."

She peeled his sweater off her face, her static filled hair stuck to her cheeks.

"I wanna take my clothes off." He undid his belt and slid it off, one loop at time. "It's getting hot in here." He sashayed towards her, hips swaying side to side. He undid the button of his jeans and pulled down his zipper, tooth by tooth. "So take off all your clothes." He grinned and rushed at her, tossed her over his shoulder and threw her on the couch.

They made love right there, christened their new home with hip hop sex in front of the naked picture window. She was sure it had sparked more than one heart attack among the geriatric neighbours.

Keep.

we call him Chief

"Morning Angus. Frank."

"Ruby, baby, you got anything with cheese?"

"I do indeed. And turkey and bacon."

"Bacon?" Frank grabbed the sandwich before Angus got hold of it. "I haven't had bacon in months."

She handed another sandwich to Angus. "Me neither. Years. I'll make it for you more often, Frank. Maybe a BLT."

Was it was time to give up the vegetarian thing? She never could go straight vegan like Gerald. Cheese and eggs always beckoned. And lately the idea of a big juicy steak tempted her. What did it matter now? There was no one in the house to tell her horror stories of slaughterhouses or the inhumanity of veal farming.

Ugh. Maybe she'd stick to vegetables a while longer.

"Nice day, Jem. Got anything good?"

"Jeremy, sweetheart. Where've you been little buddy?" She held out her arms and he fell into her, accepting a warm hug. The smell of his filth was still masked by too much cologne from his favourite pastime — hanging out in the perfume department in The Bay. She handed him tuna on whole wheat and an apple.

"I been around." He ripped open the parchment and took a huge bite. "Thought maybe I could find a cooler place to hang. You know," he poked a finger towards Angus and Frank. "Find some younger dudes." He continued to chew the first bite, then swallowed hard. "But nobody brought any food. And some Jesus guy kept hittin' us all up for redemption. I don't need no saving. I told him where to shove his bible."

She stuck a straw in a juice box and handed it to him. He finished it off in one long suck. When she first came around the park, she was shocked to find Jeremy living in the bushes. This slight young boy, no more than fourteen or fifteen. It was all she could do not the wrap him up and take him home with her. Until she learned he was a twenty-five-year-old strung out prostitute with a baby face. Instead of adopting him, she helped him get clean, took him to the free treatment program. He was ten months sober last time they talked. But he still hooked for what he called easy money. She doubted there was anything easy about it.

"You keeping on the straight and narrow?"

"Yes'm. I mean I think about it, you know. A lot. But shit nearly killed me. Not ready to be dead yet."

"Good. Let's keep it that way." She scanned the park. Still not as full as usual. And the silent one sat in the same place, same stiff, straight-backed posture as the day before. Had he even moved? She wrinkled her brow and jerked her head towards him. "What do you think of the new guy?"

"He's freaky. Never fucking moves. How does anyone do that?"

"Not sure. I can't keep still for five minutes."

"We call him Chief." Frank peeled a banana and bit half of it off at once.

"Why Chief?"

"You know." Angus tapped her on the arm. "The big scary dude in the cuckoo's nest that never talked. This guy ain't big, but he hasn't said a word in three days."

"Well, I think he's harmless." She glanced at Chief. "Did he eat his food yesterday?"

"Nah. Some magpies pecked the orange apart and a couple of yeggs took the sandwich and tried to steal his kicks. Me and Frankie, we chased 'em off."

Some of their slang had rubbed off on her. Kicks were shoes, got that. But what was a yegg?

The first two months she had started this feeding venture, she only came to the park once a week. The rest of the time she drove around town looking for any gatherings of homeless. Everyone she encountered was wary of her. They didn't turn down the food, but they eyed her with suspicion. She should have been worried for her safety, but at the time it never crossed her mind to be afraid. She was too busy looking for Gerald.

Most of the people she met stayed in groups, the majority of them men. Some of them were down on their luck, a temporary blip in their otherwise normal lives. Some were there by choice. And some had mental health issues, talking to themselves and ranting to anyone who would listen. Or to no one at all. Sometimes she'd come across families with children, living in their car or under a bridge. All walks of life, all ages, a million stories. The one thing they all had in common was hunger. Nothing else seemed to interest them. That worked for her, got her close. But sandwich bribes didn't net her any useful information about Gerald.

On the seventh week she'd pulled up to the park and loaded food into the wagon. When she turned around, she caught sight of a familiar face.

Gerald.

His hair hung down to his elbows, matted in dread-like strands. It looked like he hadn't cut it in the two years he'd been gone. His face was weathered and tanned and blanketed by a filthy beard. His clothes were torn and he wore a coat she didn't recognize. But his ebony eyes were unmistakable.

She called to him.

He looked straight at her. Or maybe through her.

She ran towards him, yelling his name, but he bolted. Adrenaline pumped through her veins and screwed with her coordination.

He vaulted over sleeping bodies and jumped a short fence.

She lost sight of him when he crashed through a copse of thick bushes. She pushed aside branches and leaves, fighting to get through the foliage. Then she heard splashing yards ahead. He was in the river. By the time she got to the bank, he was nowhere.

When she got back to her van, two of the homeless men were standing at her wagon, doling out sandwiches and fruit to the other park residents. Angus and Frank. They'd been her favourites ever since. After that, she only delivered food to that park. What if Gerald came back? What if it wasn't him at all? Maybe she'd lost her mind right alongside him.

"Jem? Jem, you listening?"

She focused her eyes. "Sorry Frank. No, I wasn't."

"I was sayin', maybe you should bring us some steak and potatoes one day, hey? Maybe a little apple pie and a nice Chianti."

"And some fava beans?" She slapped him on the back. "Keep dreaming, big boy."

She dragged the wagon around the park, handed out food and chatted with the residents. Chief's stare bore into her at every turn.

When the wagon was almost empty she approached him from the side.

"Morning. How are you today?"

Nothing.

She sighed. "I hear someone stole your breakfast yesterday." She picked up the last two sandwiches and sat on the grass in front of him. "You've got to be careful. Keep your stuff safe." She held one sandwich up in front of his face and reached toward him with the other.

He flinched.

"I'm going to tuck this into your coat. Then no one will take it from you. Okay?" She touched his coat.

He grabbed her wrist, his eyes blazed.

She froze.

He took the sandwich with his other hand without releasing his grip on her. Then nodded once, and let her go.

"Okay then." She swallowed, willing her heart to stop racing. She placed the other sandwich in front of him. "Here's one for right now. I hope you'll eat it. It's got bacon." She looked behind her, then leaned a few inches closer. "I understand it's Frank's favourite," she whispered. "But don't worry, he'd never steal from you."

She loaded the wagon into her van and slid into the driver's seat. Across the park, Chief sat stock still, like a feral animal ready to pounce. She started the van and pulled away from the curb.

Well that was a stupid move. He could have killed her on the spot. But he didn't. And maybe she broke through his hard shell, even if only the crusty top layer.

Cord Fitzbottom

"We've got to stop meeting like this." Jem grinned, one hand on her hip. Did she just flirt with him?

"I'm sorry?" Finn stood at attention on her doorstep, ready to deliver his weekly update, two thick accordion files under one arm.

"Never mind. Come on in." She walked ahead of him. "Coffee?" she called over her shoulder.

"Sure."

She pulled mugs from the cupboard above the coffee pot and glanced back at him. "Pretty casual today. Never seen you in jeans. You're usually all buttoned down."

"It's my day off. No need for suits and ties."

She spun around. "Why are you updating me on your day off? Don't you put in enough actual working hours on this case? I'm sure your wife is thrilled."

"She doesn't care."

She let her gaze rest on his lips. "I'd care."

He set the accordion files on the floor and dropped into a chair. "She left me."

"What? Oh, Finn. I'm so sorry."

"I'm not." He didn't even look up, just pulled folders and papers from one of the files.

She squinted. Guess it paid to be a cold fish in his line of work, emotions always in check.

He glanced up at her and paused. "Jem, it was more than two years ago. It's all good."

"Oh. Did I know that?"

He smiled. "I doubt it. Not exactly the kind of conversation I have with a woman when I'm investigating the disappearance of her fiancé."

"No, I guess not." She looked him up and down. "My God, are you wearing flip-flops?"

"Sorry. Would you prefer if I only came in a suit and proper shoes?"

Was he serious? "Hell no. I like you like this. You look so… civilized. Downright normal in fact." Except that every sinew of his lean frame was visible beneath his clothes. She mentally slipped his cornflower blue summer-weight sweater over his head and admired the cut of his biceps, the lump of muscle that ran from his neck to his shoulder. She imagined six-pack abs and perfect pecs. Her face flushed and she set a cup of black coffee at his clothed elbow, then turned away and waited for her cheeks to cool.

When she turned back, he had spread files and papers all over the table. It seemed a hot mess, nothing in order, a random scattering of information. Sane Gerald would have been appalled.

She sipped her coffee and scanned the case files, then pulled out a chair and sat across from him. "So what have you got?"

"Not much more than before. Except for the autopsy results." He slid a file from under some papers and flipped it open.

Jem's stomach churned. She turned her head and closed her eyes. "Are there photos?" She held her breath.

"Yes, but I left them at the precinct. You don't need to see that."

She exhaled. "Nope. Thanks."

"Okay, are you ready? Do you want to know?"

She wasn't sure what the answer was. How could you ever be ready for this? "Yes. I think so." She chewed her thumbnail. "No. No, not yet."

She pulled a bottle of brandy from the cupboard and free-poured into her coffee, then held the bottle towards Finn and raised her eyebrows.

"No thanks." He shifted in his chair and cleared his throat. "Jem, it's not even eleven."

"You're judging me?"

"No. Of course not. I apologize."

She drank half the mug and then sat again. "Okay. Now."

"He died of a gunshot wound to the chest."

She blew the air out of her lungs. "Right. You said before that he was shot."

"He had been beaten. But there were a lot of healed scars, lots of remodeled bone, so he'd suffered a few breaks. In fact, it looks like he'd taken some abuse for a while."

She leaned her elbows on the table cradled her cheeks in her hands, fingertips tapping her temples. "The only thing I knew he'd broken was his arm. The one and only time he went skiing when he was in university. Who did all that to him?"

"We don't know." He flipped the paper over. "No food in his stomach, and he was thin. Emaciated." He ran his index finger down the page. "They tested his hair for drugs. He was clean."

"You mean coke, heroin, that kind of drug?"

"I mean anything. No illegal substances. And no antipsychotics. The medical examiner said that only means the last three months. He has no idea before that."

She took a long swig of coffee. "Do you think he could have survived, alone on the streets, without his meds? For four years?"

"It's possible, but unlikely. The police psychologist agrees. He'd have been too far gone. Easy prey for any number of thugs and other street people. Which might explain some of the damage to his body." He closed the file and tossed it aside.

"The Montreal police have traced his steps back twelve months. They got a tip from a worker at a homeless shelter. He said Gerald told him he'd been staying in a treatment facility for six months, been on meds the whole time. Was doing well. He left there four months before his death. Stayed in the shelter once in a while, when it rained or on colder winter days."

Jem's shoulders quivered. She swallowed grief and drained the last of her mug. "He had the presence of mind to get help. But he never bothered to call? Never tried to come home?" She broke down in tears.

Finn kneeled on the floor beside her and crushed her in a giant hug. "Jem, he wasn't himself. He'd lost his mind. He seemed fairly lucid to the shelter worker but I bet you'd think differently. You knew him better." He sat back in the chair. "I'm going to call the doctors at the facility, find out more. But I do know that he wasn't using his real name."

"What name did he use?"

"Cord Fitzbottom."

Jem stared at Finn. She closed her eyes and conjured one brief moment eight years ago. She had been trying to convince Gerald to branch out in his clothing choices. From the time they'd met in college until that moment a year later, he'd worn nothing but corduroy pants.

"It's so 1974." She tried to shame him into denim or cargos. Hell, velvet would have been an improvement.

"But I like the way the cords fit," he argued. "You know..." He turned and stuck out his butt. "In the bottom region." Then he

33

slapped his own ass.

She'd been attracted to him from the second they almost mowed each other down in the lecture hall. She was third-year law. He was a professor exiting the hall after giving a lecture to a fresh-faced bunch of med students. He bought her a coffee and they became friends. For a year she tried to rein in her growing desire — his hair, his eyes, his brilliant mind. All so sexy. But at that ass-slapping second, she fell hopelessly in love.

She had laughed. "One point to you, Mr. Cord Fitzbottom."

He'd remembered. He couldn't have lost his entire mind.

Her legs were heavy from the brandy, her mind too fuzzy to concentrate. She refilled her mug with straight coffee.

Finn had tucked the autopsy file into the accordion folder and shuffled some of the papers. Her name typed on the label of one near the table's edge caught her attention. She picked it up and flipped it open.

"What's this?"

His cheeks blazed and he tried to snatch the folder from her hand.

"Oh no you don't. It appears to belong to me, my name on it and all." She scanned the first page and looked up at him, her jaw set. "You suspected me?"

"Standard operating procedure. Always check out the spouse."

"But we were never ma —"

"Or the girlfriend, lover. Fiancée. You know, the ones closest to the victim."

"I see." She closed the file and slid it to him with force. "And now? You still think I'm guilty?"

"Jem, I had to look into it. It's procedure." He put the folder into the file by his feet and slouched back in the chair. "I never thought you did anything to him. I had to check. For the file."

She crossed her arms. "And what did you find?"

"A huge insurance policy benefitting you if he died."

"Excuse me?"

"Gerald took out life insurance a month before he disappeared. Bought a five-year term and paid all the premiums up front. The rep told me no one's ever done that before."

She shook her head. "Why? Why wouldn't he tell me that?"

"I've no idea. But when my sergeant suggested you have him declared dead, you flat out refused. I always knew you didn't do it but that cemented it. If you were after the insurance, you would have jumped at that."

He pulled the file out and flipped through the pages, then yanked one free of the metal prongs that held it in place. He slid it across the table.

She picked it up, the thin paper like a brick in her hand. Certificate of insurance. Two-point-five-million.

"I guess you can cash that in now."

She leapt from the chair and took the stairs two at a time. Regurgitated coffee and brandy burned her throat and filled the toilet. She leaned back against the tub and sobbed.

He'd planned it. He meant to leave her. It wasn't only the crazy's fault.

"Jem?" Finn's voice echoed up the staircase. "Are you all right?"

"Yeah, I'm fine."

"Should I come back next week?"

No. Don't come back.

"Yes. Thanks."

defend the cretins

Jem awoke at five, showered and drank her coffee, made dozens of sandwiches and piled into the van to feed her homeless friends. Same thing every morning for the past week. Like she was on auto-pilot.

Work could wait. The partners were billing-hour Nazis, demanding up to eighty hours charged out per week. But when she told them Gerald had been found murdered, they shifted cases to other associates, filed motions on her behalf. They gave her time off. As much as she needed.

Was there that much time?

The park seemed in some kind of stasis. Residents that were there one day were still there the next. No more freaky new guys, only Chief, silent and still as ever. Even Jeremy stuck around to see Jem, 'his saviour,' and eat her sandwiches. Apparently she made the best sandwiches.

Frank and Angus teased and flirted with her. They gave her daily reports on the comings and goings of their little world. Chief ate what she'd left him. And Jeremy reported that Chief had pissed in the bushes by the light of the moon. He even looked like he'd put on a little weight. Her heart lightened at the sight of his less-sharp cheekbones.

She hadn't pushed her luck with Chief. Didn't want to spark an outburst, or scare him away. Not before she figured out why he wouldn't speak. So she simply said good morning and placed his food at his feet. Small steps were fine, as long as he kept eating. But she couldn't get his vacant stare out of her head. He had the look of a lost child mixed with the anger of a man who didn't want to be found. Like Gerald had looked when she chased him through that park.

She hung the certificate of insurance on her fridge with two of the tiny earth magnets Gerald liked to play with. Each morning she smoked a cigarette — only one — in the kitchen while she stared at the document. If she cashed it in, would it make her guilty of his death? Cheapen his memory? It was obvious he'd wanted her to be taken care of. Had protected her to the bitter end. His end.

One morning, after her deliveries, she tossed the empty sandwich box on the floor in the corner of the kitchen.

The shrill chime of the phone cut the silence in the house. She jumped at the intrusion. Althea, the call display announced. Jem braced herself, took one last long drag on her second cigarette that day, and clicked the talk button.

"Morning, Mother Wolfe. You're up early."

"Jemima. When is he coming home to me?"

"Finn is making the arrangements. I should know more tomorrow."

Silence on the other end. "Finn? New boyfriend already?"

Wow. Jem rubbed the back of her neck and twisted it side to side until a loud crack relieved some tension. "Detective Finn Wight. He's the man that's spent four years looking for your son."

"And you're on a first name basis with this detective?"

"Four years, Althea. Dozens of meetings, even more phone calls. That and the subject matter lends itself to a little familiarity." Jem snatched another cigarette and lit it with the matches she'd picked up at the grocery store. "What do you want?" She rubbed her temples and shut her eyes.

"I want to make arrangements for my only child to be buried with dignity." Althea's voice cracked and soft muffled sobs came through the receiver.

"I know. I'm sorry. But he doesn't want to be buried, he wants to be cremated."

"He's my son. I think I know what he'd want. I've been in touch with my pastor to perform the eulogy. Or are you going to tell me that's wrong too?"

Of course it was wrong. Gerald was an atheist. But he'd never had the balls to tell his mother that.

Jem curled her lips around her teeth and bounced in place. "No ma'am. You plan the funeral exactly the way you want it." No point in arguing. She was going to do it her way anyway.

"Do you have his will?"

Jem hesitated. She hadn't thought of a will. "No. I don't know if there is one."

"Aren't you his lawyer?"

"No, I'm not." Jem held the phone between her ear and shoulder and thumbed through a stack of mail she'd been ignoring. "I'm a criminal defense attorney. I don't do wills and estates."

"Right. You defend the cretins that rob and steal and murder people. Like my son."

Jem took a deep breath and shook her head. "I defend innocent people wrongly accused. And I think I have to hang up now. Because the one truth that I know today, Althea, is that I no longer have to put up with any of your crap." She pressed the end button hard, then poked it several times with her index finger. It didn't have the same satisfying feel as an old-fashioned slamming of the receiver.

She had to call Dean. He and Gerald were best friends since

junior high school, research partners, golf buddies. He'd know if Gerald had a will. She should have called him the day she found out, not chickened out and waited two weeks. He'll be devastated. This was going to be the hardest call to make.

She dialed Finn's private cell number. In typical cop-on-the-ball fashion, he picked up on the first ring.

"Jem? Is everything all right?"

"Yes, fine. Althea's hot to trot to bury her son and I think I hung up on her. If I text you her number, will you deal with her about transporting the body?" She should feel terrible about fobbing her future mother-in-law off on this kind man, but she didn't. Then again, Althea was no longer her future anything-in-law.

"Sure, I can do that. I'll see you tomorrow?"

Her chest was heavy, her heart pressed on her stomach. "Is there anything big? Can we skip a week?"

Silence. Had his phone dropped the call? She shifted her feet. "Finn?"

"Sorry. Of course. Overwhelmed?"

"For years and years."

"I'll see you next week. Call if you need anything."

"Thanks. I will."

No she wouldn't. She'd been dealing with everything alone for so long, she didn't need anything from anyone.

she can't have the house

"No will? Dean, are you sure?" Jem held the phone in a vice grip.

"He never told me about one. Do you know if he has a lawyer?"

She should know this stuff. Why didn't she know this stuff? "No, I don't know. He doesn't have a safe deposit box. Didn't leave any notes." She glanced around the kitchen, paused her gaze at the credenza that doubled for a filing cabinet. "I'll have to go through the papers I have here. Is there anything in his office?"

"I'll look. But it shouldn't matter. You lived together for six years, you're common-law, right?"

"Technically we lived together for two years. In law, we've been separated for four. He did leave, after all." Althea may be deemed the sole living heir.

"What about the house, Dean? She can't have the house."

"No, she can't have the house, Jem. You're on the title, joint ownership. At most she might ask to be paid for his half. But you know more about this stuff than me. Can you look into it? Call a colleague?"

She clutched the phone and took a deep breath. "Yes, I can do that. Don't know what the fucking old bat would want any of it for anyway, she's on her bloody deathbed."

"Jeez, Jem, I doubt she wants to take your home away." There was a long pause. "Are you all right?"

She sighed. "No, but yeah. Sorry. But she's been such a bitch. Worse since he went missing. Hell on wheels since he died." Was that why the all the insurance? It would be the one thing his mother couldn't touch. "Dean, are you all right? I'm so sorry to mix the bad news with such morbid talk about wills and stuff. And really sorry I didn't step up on the day I found out. I should have called you."

"I understand. What's another two weeks when it's been almost four years?" The sounds of his breath and of him scratching his chin, his giveaway nervous tick, filled the receiver. "I always figured he'd walk through the lab door one day like nothing ever happened. Like nothing had changed."

Jem stared at the leaded glass of the front door. "I know. That's what I hoped for too."

drown in cheesecake

Bacon sizzled in the cast iron skillet and flooded Jem's head with memories of home. Her senior year of high school. Those lazy Saturday mornings when her father would be up before dawn to read the paper and finish off an entire pot of coffee to himself. He would make a big family breakfast. She would wake to the sizzle of bacon, its aroma mixed with the wonderful smell of frying onions. Cheese and onion omelets with crispy, just-this-side-of-burned, bacon and thick, white toast drenched in butter and honey.

No wonder he died so young.

She used a fork to scoop the crispy strips from the pan, like her father had done. They rested on paper towels while she cut two dozen tomatoes into thick slices.

The bacon beckoned, called her by name, broke her will power. Saliva pooled in her mouth. She swallowed it, sneaked a piece from the pile and snapped the end off with her teeth.

She let the warm meat sit on her tongue. The salt brought more saliva. She crunched into the crisp wonder of it, crushed the bacon between her teeth and tilted her head back.

"Oh my God."

She stuffed the whole piece in her mouth and chased it with three more. When she picked up a fifth, Gerald's face appeared in front of her. His lecture on nitrates and salt and fat played in her head. She closed her eyes against the phantom of her dead fiancé only to be bombarded with images he'd been kind enough to share with her. Pigs hanging from their hind feet, their necks slit at the carotid while still alive and squealing. Was that really how it was done?

The bacon turned on her and rose up in her throat. She spun around and vomited every glorious bite into the sink.

When would she give up this guilt? Why couldn't she bring herself to do anything he didn't approve of? He was dead for crying out loud. She could make her own choices now. Eat as much meat as she wanted. Drown herself in cheesecake and white bread if she felt like it. Have nothing but ice cream and potato chips for dinner. Not alphabetize the CDs. Leave water rings all over the wood.

"You happy, Gerald?" she yelled into the empty kitchen. "You're going to haunt me for life." She leaned one hand on the cupboard, the other on her hip and scowled at the room. Then she burst out laughing. "Oh shit. Jemima Gertrude Stone, it's your turn to lose your freaking mind."

BLTs and PTSD

One thing Jem had learned about homeless folk, they have no pretention about food. They'd eat whatever you gave them as long as they weren't allergic. And they all loved bacon.

Frank and Angus scarfed down those sandwiches so fast she thought they'd both choke. Jeremy was a bit more civilized except for when he chatted with her between bites without swallowing. But like hell was she going to lecture anyone in the park on proper table manners. There were no tables.

"I think the guy's schizo." Jeremy wiped his mouth on his sleeve and gestured to Chief with one thumb.

Angus elbowed him in the ribs. "Shush now about that stuff." He flashed a weak smile. "Sorry, Ruby."

"It's okay." She knew from schizo. And the only sign Chief showed was being mute. "Why do you think so Jeremy?"

"Because he's nuts!"

"Well, there are lots of forms of nuts. Some people think I'm nuts for coming out here and feeding you all every morning."

"Do you think you're nuts?"

"Hell no. I think it's the sanest thing I've ever done."

Jeremy nodded and snickered through his BLT-filled mouth.

She watched Chief take tentative bites from the sandwich. He pulled the bacon out and ate it first. Then the tomato. Then he ate each triangular piece of bread. Methodical. Curious. Purposeful. No, he didn't appear schizophrenic. "I think he may have suffered PTSD."

"STD? You think he's got herpes or something?"

She laughed and shook her head. "Oh hell, Jeremy, you crack me up. PTSD. Post-traumatic stress disorder. It's like shock, only a million times worse."

"You mean maybe he's an army guy? Fucked up by the war or something?

"Maybe. I don't know."

But not knowing was eating at her. She knew the stories of every other park resident. But Chief remained an enigma.

nirvana

Jem sipped at a cup of chai tea sweetened with fireweed honey while Finn settled in for their overdue weekly chat. He looked right at home at her kitchen table. That shouldn't be surprising, he'd been there often enough. It was possible he'd spent more time in the house than Gerald. Was it weird that Finn's presence made her so happy?

He pulled one folder from the accordion file and set it in front of him. She wasn't sure she could handle more murder talk at that moment.

Jem tapped the side of her cup with one fingernail. "Why'd she leave you?"

Finn hesitated. "I beg your pardon?"

"Your wife. What happened?"

"Does that matter?"

"No. I'm just curious." She ran her index finger around the rim of her cup, then met his eyes. "You know more about me than most of my friends. Maybe more than I even know you do. But all I know about you is that you're very sweet, a damn good cop, divorced." She grinned and raised one eyebrow. "And tall, dark and handsome."

His cheeks pinked.

"Fair enough." He stood, removed his suit jacket and hung it over the back of the chair. Two long strides and he was across the room. He put the kettle on the burner and lit the gas.

Right at home.

He pulled a mug from the cupboard and a teabag from the canister next to the fridge, tossed the bag into the mug and leaned against the counter, one leg crossed over the other, his palms on the countertop. Whenever she did that, the edge of the faux-granite was icy on the small of her back. It intersected him mid-butt. And he wasn't even standing up straight.

"It's a common problem on the job."

"That's it? Just the job?"

"There were a couple of cases that got the better of me. I put in a lot of extra hours on one in particular. It robbed her of my attention." He crossed his arms and shook his head. "She was jealous. Of a case. Ridiculous."

"What's she like?"

"Bitch on wheels."

"Ouch. You had to love her once, right?" She smirked and cocked her head. "You didn't marry for money did you, Detective?"

He snickered and shook his head. The kettle whistled. He pushed himself to his feet and filled the cup with steaming water. He bobbed the teabag up and down in the mug and sat at the table.

"No. I did love her. Years ago. But she changed. I guess we all change." He bounced the teabag up and down in the mug then took a tentative sip. "We met in high school."

"Don't tell me. You were the star quarterback, she was the head cheerleader."

He flinched.

"I'm sorry, Finn. I didn't mean that."

"Amy was on the debate team. They won regionals every year she lead them, but her bitter disappointment was never placing better than fifth at nationals. She was valedictorian. Studied humanities in university. She was vibrant and alive. I don't know what happened after we married, but it all ended. She never did anything. No career, no job. Hell she didn't even volunteer or join a book club. She waited for me to get home. Was pissed when I was late, pissed when I got called out on my off hours. It's my job, you know? My life. She never understood it."

"Kids?"

"No. She also waited around hoping to get pregnant. It never happened. We were going to see a fertility specialist but she left first. Probably for the best." He blew on his tea, took another sip and stared into the mug, his eyes glistening. "I couldn't give a child enough attention."

So much for cold fish. Were there more layers under that muscular, business-like exterior?

"So." He picked up the file and tapped the edge against the table. "Let's talk about the case."

"Can we call it something else?"

"What do you mean?"

"'The Case.' Sounds so clinical. So cold. We need a code word."

His eyes softened. "All right. Like what?"

"Nirvana."

His brow furrowed but he smiled. "Okay. Why?"

"Because that's where I imagine Gerald is. We aren't religious people, don't believe in heaven. But I want to think he's somewhere perfect. Where there is no pain, no hunger, no murder. No crazy." She wiped the back of her hand across her cheek. "And he loved Kurt Cobain."

Finn reached across the table and squeezed her hand. "Let's talk about nirvana."

Her fingers tingled under his hand. She looked into his eyes and a pang sliced through her chest. She glanced at her teacup. "If we must," she whispered.

Finn slid a plastic bag across the table. Bright red evidence tape sealed it shut. Her grandmother's clunky platinum ring with the black pearl mounted in the centre rested inside.

Her throat closed. She reached for the bag but he pulled it away.

"Sorry, Jem. It's still evidence."

the ring

Jem spent a sleepless night playing, rewinding, and replaying what Finn had told her that evening.

Gerald had lied to the treatment facility. Lied to the doctor. About everything. Where he lived, what his real name was, what prior treatment he'd had. Even about his first psychotic break. But could he lie? Was it lying when he had such a tenuous grasp on reality?

The one constant was the others. They still spoke to him. Still guided his decisions. They stole him from her.

They weren't voices in his head. That's what his doctor had told her after the first assessment. To him it was real. Voices that spoke to him from the television, the walls, his computer, the pencil in his hand. But most often they spoke from her grandmother's ring that she used to wear on her right ring finger.

A month before he disappeared, they were curled up on the sofa together. It was a rare moment of doing nothing, accomplishing nothing. Just being. While they watched a forgettable old movie, he brought her hand up and held it next to his face. Displays of his love had become rarer and rarer. He'd started his meds again a few days before, so she attributed the sudden affection to antipsychotics getting his brain back to normal, bringing her Gerald home.

He kissed her ring and hugged it to his ear. When she realized he wasn't kissing and cuddling, but whispering and listening, she yanked her hand away and twisted in his arms to look at him.

"What are you doing?"

"Can I have your hand back? I have to hear." His eyes were wild and sweat beaded on his brow and his upper lip.

"You stopped your medication again, didn't you?"

He stared at her. His mouth moved but no words formed.

She'd hid the ring at the bottom of her underwear drawer. One less outlet from which the others could contact him. Weeks after he disappeared she went to put the ring on again, but it had disappeared along with him.

The doctor Finn spoke to in Montreal said Gerald wore an antique ring. He often held it to his ear and whispered into the pearl. The medical examiner found it lodged in his throat. The police surmised that when he was robbed he tried to hide it, to protect it. But she knew it wasn't the ring he was protecting. It was the others.

She had always loved that ring, the one reminder of a grandmother who'd died when Jem was too young to remember her with clarity. But could she ever put it on her finger again? Would the others try to speak to her? No, that was ridiculous. The voices may not have been inside his head, but his head is where they were born. Not hers.

Gerald's illness had robbed her of so much. Time, happiness, peace of mind. She'd often questioned her own sanity.

She peeked at the clock. Four-forty-seven. Her room was bathed in darkness, the sun still forty minutes from cresting the horizon. She tossed the covers off and made her way downstairs.

She stared at the insurance form still Bucky-balled to the refrigerator, drank a coffee, and sucked on a cigarette. Her new morning ritual. And not a healthy or productive one either.

Time to shake things up.

She pulled the insurance certificate from the fridge and opened her laptop. It wasn't hard to find the forms she needed to make the claim. One call to Finn to get the death certificate and another to the office to make an appointment with a notary, and it was done. She would cash in. That's what he wanted. She would give him that.

mine are dead

She pulled into her usual spot in front of the park. The residents came at her from all directions. She stepped out of the van and slid the side door open.

"Morning everybody. What a reception."

"Where ya been, Ruby? It's gotta be after ten."

"Sorry Angus. Had something I had to take care of. But I brought treats today to make up for it."

She handed sandwiches and drinks to everyone. And a brownie.

"What?" Jeremy squealed and clapped. "Oh my, oh my. No fruit?"

"Fruit too." She leaned into the van and pulled out two reusable grocery bags. "You want to hand out the oranges for me?"

"Can I have another brownie?"

"If there are enough, you can."

"Deal." He tucked his food into the side pockets of his oversized jacket, gathered up the bags and traipsed through the park distributing fruit to the other residents. He chatted with each of them, his hands doing more talking than his mouth. He made a wide berth around Chief.

She pulled a smaller bag from behind the now-empty box, closed the van and crossed the park. Chief sat at attention in the shrub, his face an emotionless mask.

"Good morning. How are you doing today?"

He answered her the same way he did every day. With silence.

"Well, I've had better days." She sat cross-legged in front of him and rolled down the edges of the bag. "Tuna on rye today, and an orange. I already cut it in wedges so you don't have to peel it." She set those in front of him and unfolded the parchment to reveal his breakfast. She pulled the straw from a drinking box of chocolate milk, released it from its cellophane wrapper and poked it into the silver hole. She set that next to the sandwich.

He eyed the food and glanced at her. He inched one arm out from its protected spot under his armpit, picked up one half of the tuna and took a small nibble. He chewed once, then followed right away with a bigger bite.

Until now he would wait until she walked away before he'd start eating. A sign of trust perhaps? Or was it only because he was as hungry as the rest of them? At least the need for food, the will to survive, outweighed his silent posturing. Definite progress.

She scanned the park while he chewed and swallowed. Most every resident was fixated on the drama of her interactions with Chief. He'd made quite the impression on all of them. Had they set aside their wariness and become as concerned for him as they were for each other? She had proven he was not a threat. But she still had no idea who he was or why he was there. Or why he wouldn't speak.

"Do you have family?"

He stopped sucking on the milk and turned to stone.

"Mine are dead. All of them."

His eyes went cold.

She should shut the hell up. Not press too many buttons at once. But she needed to talk to someone. Her friends had all but abandoned her in the past two years. She couldn't talk to Althea about anything. Cecilia just wanted to get her laid. There was Finn.

But she didn't want to talk case files and fingerprints. She needed to just talk. To someone. Anyone.

"Dad died when I was a kid. Eighteen. Okay, maybe that's not a kid, legally speaking. But I still needed my daddy, you know?"

Sucking sounds filled her ears. Chief drained his milk box, the wonderful noise of the last drops being pulled through the straw like music in the air.

"Here, I brought you another."

He took care in pulling the straw free of its tether and poking it through the hole. Then he sucked on it until the same end-of-milk sounds came.

Jem held out her hands and he placed both cartons in her palms. She set them beside her. "Do you like brownies?" She handed him a small parchment wrapped package.

He took a bite from the corner and glanced at her. He didn't smile. Didn't speak. But there was silent appreciation.

"So, I was telling you about my dad. He had a heart attack. At the kitchen table. Forty-two years old." She stared past Chief's head at a lone blue blossom in the bush. "I was working at the time, summer job before university. Mom found him. He was crumpled on the linoleum, fried egg and bacon all over the table and floor. He'd pulled his breakfast plate off when he keeled over. I always thought it was his way of saying, look, the bacon did it. I was killed by bad breakfast choices." She smirked and looked at her hands. "He was you know. Bad food. Bad cholesterol. Clogged arteries. Early death." She wiped tears from her cheeks.

"They were high school sweethearts, Mom and Dad. And happy all through their relationship. How rare is that? I mean they fought and all, who doesn't? But happy. So rare." She resisted the urge to grab the cigarettes from her van. She needed to quit again, before she suffered the same fate as her father.

"Mom wasn't herself after he died. Then I moved away to go to university. Mom withdrew, couldn't cope with being alone. I like to think she died of a broken heart, but really, she killed herself. Overdosed on sleeping pills." She tugged one blade of grass from the ground and pulled it between her thumb and index finger, then snapped it in half and dropped it.

"It could have been an accident, right? She took those pills every night after he died, sometimes two or three when one wasn't enough to dull the pain. Maybe she needed just a couple more." She huffed and shook her head. "But the cops said no. She took the whole damn bottle, washed them down with a tumbler of scotch. Suicide."

Jem leaned back and stretched her legs out on the grass. She hadn't told anyone but Gerald about that. "I've felt like an orphan ever since. No parents, no brothers and sisters. That's what I had in common with Gerald. Dead dad and only child. But you have no clue who Gerald is, so I'm going to leave you alone now."

She pulled the second sandwich from the bag and tucked it inside Chief's jacket. "For later," she whispered. "You like the brownies? I made them yesterday. I saved two more for you." She placed them at his feet.

She gathered the trash into her lap and hesitated. "I'd like to know your name. Can you tell me that?"

Nothing.

"Okay. Maybe another day." She looked over her shoulder across the park. "They call you Chief. Did you know that? I hope it doesn't bother you. They mean it with a modicum of respect."

Nothing.

She stood and patted him on the shoulder. "See you tomorrow, Chief. Thanks for listening."

what about love?

Jem ran down the stairs zipping up the side of her summer dress. She swung the door open the second the bell chimed for the third time. "You're late."

Finn stood on her doorstep. The evening sun bathed him in orange light. All buttoned up again.

"Sorry. Is it too late? We could reschedule."

"No, it's fine. I'm only teasing."

They sat at the table in the same seats they always chose. It had become a ritual, this weekly meeting. Part of the fabric of her life. Like a really lame recurring date with no romance, no touching. No sex. Except the stuff she made up in her head.

What would she do every Saturday if Gerald's murder got solved?

Finn rubbed a palm over his long crew cut. He needed a trim. It was on the verge of falling out of line, not standing at attention. A vision of a long-haired Finn flashed through her mind. She covered her smile with one hand. He'd be even hotter with long hair.

"I don't have much news tonight. I can't tell you everything, being a murder investigation and all."

"I understand. Not sure I could handle everything."

"I bet you can handle more than you think." He pulled out a notebook and pencil. He tap-tap-tapped the eraser end against the paper. "What was Gerald like?"

"What do you mean?

"At home. Everyday Gerald. Who was he?"

"Why does that matter?"

"I don't know. I'm no profiler, but maybe his everyday habits, the person he was at home when he's most vulnerable, not the public guy all his colleagues know, will tell us something about why he left. About where he went. Maybe point to why he went there. If we knew that, it might lead to the killer."

Jem nodded slowly and looked past Finn's head at the wall. Gerald's write-on wipe-off calendar still hung there, frozen in time, four years ago this June. His neat black Xs through the first to the fourth, obsessively marking the passage of time. Commemorating his successful completion of each listed task. Then on the fifth, the X was not so neat. An arrow of red marker shoved an incomplete task into the box for the sixth. The X through the sixth was only a slash, not confined to the square allocated for that twenty-four hour period, but invading the territory of the twelfth. Two tasks were circled and moved from the seventh all the way to the fifteenth. Messy, crooked slashes marked the seventh to the tenth. The eleventh was a dark square, obliterated by black Sharpie. And then nothing. He didn't come home on the twelfth.

Maybe the slash from the sixth pushed him over the edge. How could he face his precious calendar after the sixth declared war on his mind?

"He was obsessed with order. Numerical, alphabetical, chronological. But he never ironed his clothes and rarely brushed out his hair." She shifted her gaze to Finn's angular face. "He was obsessed with health food. No meat, no eggs, no cheese. Nothing that caused any animal any discomfort. But he refused to get a pet. Wouldn't go near the SPCA. He was obsessed with finding a cure for all cancers, a magic bullet if you will. But he refused to take any medication if he got a cold or the flu. And of course, he went off his meds. You know, the antipsychotics."

"He was a walking contradiction."

Could he read her mind? "Yes, that's what I always told him. He was brilliant, a genius. But he didn't understand the simplest, most obvious humour. A complete social nerdlinger." She huffed. "That sounds like such a stereotype. He wasn't completely awkward. I mean he never had trouble finding a girlfriend. And I know he loved me. But he didn't believe in public displays of affection." No, he kept those very private. And then even the private ones became rare.

"All right. What about daily habits? How did he spend his time?"

"Five a.m., run. Five forty-five, shower. Six, coffee, soy yoghurt, fresh fruit, and low-fat granola. In the lab by seven, tirelessly researching to find ways to cure his mother. Six p.m. shower number two. Seven, dinner. Eight, well, between then and his ten forty-five strict bed time, that was his 'flex time' as he called it."

"What did he do then, TV, surf the internet, drink with the boys?"

She snorted. "Uh, no. Read medical journals, putter in his herb garden, clean something, anything, everything."

"I see." Finn made some notes then tap-tap-tapped the eraser on the paper again. "When did he spend time with you?"

"We got up together. Sometimes showered together. Coffee and breakfast and dinner, if I was home. Once in a blue moon, flex time did include just being together, just hanging out. If we did go out, it was to some fundraising event, or the occasional awards ceremony. Once a year we went to my office party. We were both busy with careers. Our lives only intersected at meals and at bedtime."

"Is that why no kids?"

"I suppose. We talked about it, but it never seemed to be the right time."

"Was your life with him always like this?"

She smiled and shook her head. "Not when I was in university. He lectured there. That's how we met. He was older, six years. Back then he was a lot more… let's say normal." As normal as a genius with a career trajectory that pretty much guaranteed him a place in the cancer research history books can be. "He wasn't as fastidious. Didn't alphabetize his CDs or mark time on the calendar. Didn't make lists."

"When did that change?"

"It could have been going on for years. But I didn't notice until we moved in together. Bought this house. That was when he started getting paranoid, thinking there was some phantom group trying to steal his research. It started with stuff like 'they' are reading his emails, or 'they' are tapping his phone. Soon it was 'the others.' Those were the voices he heard. The others spoke to him from everywhere. But his main connection to them was my grandmother's pearl ring. When he started listening to the pearl and whispering into it, I knew whatever was going on was very, very wrong."

Her mind wandered to Chief. Did he hear voices too? Maybe the shrub was some conduit to whoever was telling him to keep quiet and not go home. Wherever the hell home was.

She tapped her fingernails on the table. "I've done some research into Gerald's disease since he left. He always said oranges had been genetically modified because they started to taste like apples. And the water that came out of the taps in his apartment — before we moved in together — smelled of gas. I didn't smell it, and oranges tasted the same. I found out later those were signs." She sucked on her front teeth. "Those, and when he thought the Chinook winds spoke his name, kept seeing a dog in the lab at the university in his peripheral vision. The same dog all the time. He used to laugh at himself, said he must be going senile." She shook her head. "Nope, not senile. They were just more indicators of the shit storm to come. According to Dean, all that had been going on for years."

Jem pushed her chair away from the table and put her hands on her thighs. "I need wine. You want some?"

"Sure. Why not?"

"You know what?" She eyed the indigo digits on the stove that offered an eerie glow to the darkening room. Almost eight o'clock. "It's getting late and I'm starved."

"Oh, yeah. All right." He rushed to gather papers and tucked them into the file. "I'll get out of your hair. Maybe I can come back tomorrow?"

She poured two glasses of wine and placed one in front of him. There hadn't been many visitors the past two years. Most people didn't know what to say, how to act. Jokes might be misconstrued, simple turns of phrase took on ominous meanings. The unwavering support wavered. The daily check-ins from friends and family became weekly, then monthly, then almost non-existent. Having someone stay for more than ten minutes, even if the topic was her dead lover, was a comfort.

"No, I don't mean leave. I mean — do you like spaghetti?"

"Yeah, I love it." His eyes seemed backlit against the dusk, his smile warm and genuine.

"Great. You can make the garlic toast."

Jem pulled the pasta pot from a deep drawer, set it in the sink and turned on the tap. "Bread's on the counter, margarine in the fridge. Garlic pot is left of the blender."

"Yes ma'am. I'm on it. Margarine?"

"Gerald's old vegan habits die hard I guess."

Gerald had loved to cook. She was always in his way when he had control of the stove and the knives and the vegetables. When he had control of himself. He was a master, each component of a meal, each course all ready and served in perfect time. Nothing undercooked. No soggy noodles, never a burned carrot. Perfect.

She'd managed to feed them both in his decline, when he couldn't connect with his love of cooking. Couldn't connect with her. She ate nothing but take-out early in his disappearance. If she never saw another pizza again it would be too soon. But she'd figured out the kitchen and cooked for herself in the years since. She took command. She was now the master. Or at least not a total bumbling fool.

Finn's presence in her arena brought nerves bubbling to the surface, as if Gerald was back and she wasn't good enough to share the space. Except that Finn was nothing like Gerald. For one thing he took up twice as much room. And he didn't shuffle her aside and take over her tasks. Even so, she was tempted to sit and drink while he made dinner for them both.

What would Gerald think of another man in his kitchen? The fact that Finn was using his utensils would be far worse than discovering that she'd spent so much time with the detective. Worse than knowing she couldn't deny a growing attraction to him.

Gerald never was the jealous type. Not when it came to Jem.

She moved about the small kitchen dancing an awkward music-free waltz with Finn, vying for floor space and counter room. Hyper-aware of his presence, she did everything she could to keep her distance.

Finn scooted behind her and reached for the fridge door. His leg brushed her dress, shifting it around her rear before the hem settled at the back of her knees. He reached over her shoulder and plucked a bulb of garlic from the pot. His whole body invaded her space, subtle cologne filled her head. He sidled two feet away, snatching a paring knife from the knife block on the way. He was comfortable in the kitchen. In her kitchen.

When the pasta was *al dente* and the sauce bubbled in the pan, he pulled the garlicky bread from the broiler and set it on the counter. She tossed pasta with sauce then sprinkled fresh parsley and shaved parmesan over top. Every time she shot a glance his direction he was staring at her. When she pulled plates from the overhead cupboard, staring. When she fumbled with the forks and they clattered to the counter, staring.

She tugged her dress down and smoothed her hair. "Have a seat. Please. More wine?"

"Sure." He sat and continued to watch while she dished up their plates. He slid steaming garlic toast on the side. "Just a fork?"

"Sorry, do you want a spoon? I never did learn to eat it that way. Any time I try, the spoon usually ends up flying in the air and splashing sauce all over the table."

"So how do you roll it?"

"Like this." She stabbed the fork into a shallow pile of pasta until stainless hit the plate. She twirled the fork until the right amount of noodles clung to the tines, lifted the fork and shoved it in her mouth. Errant pasta strands were slurped through pursed lips. The tail end of the noodles whipped up and slapped the tip of her nose.

He leaned back and laughed. "Very ladylike. Okay, let me try." Most of the pasta fell from the fork before it hit his mouth. He slurped anyway, and ended up with sauce on his nose, one cheek, and dripping down his chin.

"Good job, sir. It takes years of practice to perfect that technique, but you picked it up first try." Jem reached across and wiped his chin and nose with her napkin, then froze on the way to his cheek. Her face warmed. She pulled away and shifted her gaze to her plate. "Sorry."

"It's all right. That was nice."

They ate in silence, discomfort like a Plexiglas wall between them. Or maybe that barrier was only in front of her. Each time she glanced up, he was watching her and smiling. He was different since the night he told her Gerald was dead. Relaxed. Human.

"So. Now what?"

She looked up. "Now what, what?"

"For you, Jem. Now what? He's gone. You've spent all this time on hold, waiting for him. Waiting for an end. Now what?"

"I don't want to think about it. I'm going to just get up each day and see where life takes me."

"Still feeding the homeless every morning? I get why you started, but he's not out there anymore. You won't find him. Why keep doing it?"

"Because of the rest of them. It stopped being about him and became about them. They need me. I can't abandon them, now can I?"

"No, I suppose not." He broke his bread over the plate now empty of noodles and sopped up the remaining sauce, shoving a large piece of toast in his mouth. He was not a dainty eater. He chased the food with the rest of his wine and filled both of their glasses.

He cleared his throat. "Are you finding happiness?"

"Sometimes." She held his gaze for two seconds before she had to turn away. She stood and took their plates, turned her back on him and put the plates on the counter. She squeezed soap and ran the water until glistening bubbles crested the rim of the sink, then slid the dishes beneath the suds.

His chair squeaked against the tiles. One muscular arm reached around her and placed the pasta bowl at her elbow.

No, she hadn't found any happiness. Not until tonight.

He leaned against the counter, bread and garlic forced back by his hips, his arms crossed against his chest. "What about love?" His voice had a softer quality than usual.

Finn pushed a strand of hair from her cheek and tucked it behind her ear. "You're young. Beautiful. Brilliant. Any guy would be lucky to have you. Maybe it's time to look for that kind of happiness again."

She stared at him in silence. She'd thought about it many times. When Gerald had been missing more than a year she started taking notice of other men. When she lost hope she would ever see him again, loneliness consumed her and everything had a bitter, jaded edge. But no matter how long he was gone, no matter how nuts he was when he left, the mere thought of it smacked of betrayal. Disrespect. What if being with another erased the gorgeous, formerly sane man she loved from her memory banks? What if he came home and she'd been unfaithful? She couldn't do that to him. Even though he'd abandoned her without as much as a goodbye.

"Jem?" Finn's long fingers grazed her arm.

She snapped out of her daze. For the first time since she'd met him, he looked vulnerable.

His eyes locked on hers. He licked his upper lip then scraped his bottom teeth across it. He took a deep breath. "What about me?"

She blinked hard. "You?"

"Look, I know we've only ever talked about Gerald. Every time we've met, every conversation we've had. It's all been clues and leads, questions and hard truths. Pain, coping, grieving. But Jem." He stepped towards her and took one soapy hand in his. "I've grown very fond of you."

She felt like a high school nerd being asked to prom by the star quarterback. Until Gerald died, she'd never looked at Finn as anything except the tough-but-kind cop who was searching for the man she loved. He was handsome, sexy. That was hard to miss. But not her normal type. And she was certain she wasn't his.

She stared at his tan face, the furrows between his trimmed brows. The deep green flecks in his pale blue eyes. The dimple that dented only one cheek, even when he wasn't smiling. Why hadn't she noticed that before?

He bent his head towards her but stopped shy of a kiss.

She froze. It had been more than four years since a man had stood so close. Since her heart fluttered and her legs flushed with warmth. Gerald had only been dead for a month. This was not a good idea. She was not ready for love. Not romance. Her breasts hollowed and then filled the cups of her bra with each heavy breath. Maybe three glasses of wine had muddied her judgment.

Screw love and romance. But sex? Hell yeah, she could handle some of that.

She tipped her head back, threw her arms around his neck and crushed her lips to his.

His hands went up her back and entwined in her hair at the nape of her neck. He smelled of wine and cologne and musky, sweet sweat. She pushed her body against his hard form, her breasts pressed against his torso.

He slid his lips down her face, along her jaw line, then feasted on her neck. The stubble of his nine o'clock shadow scratched at her delicate skin and sent a shockwave aching through her body.

Four years. Four damn years.

She tugged his shirt free of his belted waistband and slid her hands along his smooth skin, from his waist up to his broad back. She couldn't stop herself. Didn't want to. She fumbled his belt open and popped the button of his pants.

He stopped kissing her neck, pulled back and looked into her eyes, his breath heavy.

He shoved the bread aside. Garlic bulbs skittered across the counter. The margarine tub slid and landed in the dishwater. He tucked his hands under her armpits and lifted her with little effort. He sat her on the countertop, reached under her dress and peeled off her underwear. His pants landed at his ankles, the belt buckle clanged against the adobe floor. His eyes locked on hers and he pulled her towards him.

"Finn, wait."

His brow creased. "But…"

"Condom?"

"Oh shit." He stooped down, pulled his wallet from the back pocket of his pants and fished out a shiny packet.

A grown man who kept a rubber in his wallet. Interesting. Had he known she'd be this easy? Or maybe just hoped so. And who the hell cared anyway?

He rolled on the condom. His fingers trembled and fumbled with the latex.

She wrapped her legs around his body and pulled him into her before he even finished. He took one ass cheek in each hand, slid her to the edge of the counter, and kissed her.

She devoured his mouth, the wine and garlic that lingered on his tongue better than any dessert.

She gripped the edge of the counter with both hands, his thrusts coming fast and hard. Her head bounced off the pine cupboard behind her and she laughed.

He picked her up, stepped out of his pants and carried her to the living room, never leaving her body, kissing her all the way. He kneeled on the area rug and laid her down as light as a feather. Then he shifted gears, made each movement long and slow, nearly withdrawing, then filling her with each push.

Every rhythmic thrust arched her spine and tilted her head back. He drew out her pleasure, maximized her enjoyment, took her to the brink and then stalled again and again before sending her over the top. He was in full control of himself. And of her.

His movements intensified, shorter, faster, deeper. Sparkles of light exploded behind her closed eyelids, her heartbeat pounded in her ears. Was that her screaming?

He pulled her into him while pushing hard against her and stopped fully inside.

Her arms dropped to the rug, her legs as limp as the spaghetti they'd shared.

He collapsed on top of her, his gasping breath rasped in her ear.

They lay still for minutes, their sweat mingling where his forehead rested against her collarbone. She ran her hands over his crew cut and drew a finger behind one ear.

He propped up on his elbows. "Wow."

She laughed. "Yeah, you could say that."

He buried his face in her cleavage and sighed.

"Finn?"

"Mm-hmm?"

"Was it Gerald's case you obsessed over? The one that ended your marriage?"

He lifted his head and looked at her for a few seconds. He nodded once.

She swallowed and brushed the back of her fingers across his lips and up to his temple. "Was it because of Gerald?"

A quick huff of air from his nostrils tickled her collarbone. The tips of his mouth turned up in a slight curl. "No. Not because of Gerald."

I fixed you two

Jem sat in front of Chief and watched him nibble at the egg salad on whole wheat. "Not your favourite?"

Chief glanced up at her and shrugged.

"I mentioned Gerald yesterday. Do you mind if I talk about him?"

Another shrug.

"Gerald is my fiancé. Or at least he was. He disappeared about four years ago. He's dead. They found him last month." Sorrow welled up in her core, constricted her throat, and threatened to unleash more tears. She set her jaw and looked at her hands clasped in her lap.

"He was paranoid schizophrenic." She looked at Chief. "Do you know what that is?"

His eyes released their squint for a split second.

"He disappeared one day. I still don't know why. He was off his meds and he was hearing voices. And he was erratic as hell, all over the map with emotions and anger then complete and utter exhaustion followed by hyperactive bouts of energy." She let the tears come. "I miss him," she whispered. Not crazy Gerald. She missed sane Gerald. The man she fell in love with. Before he became fastidious Gerald. Before the devolution of his brilliant mind. She wiped her nose with the back of her hand and then wiped it on the grass. "I wish he could come home."

She reached out and took one of Chief's filthy hands. "Do you have family? Is there someone looking for you, wondering where you are? Someone who wants you to come home?"

Tears pooled in the corners of his eyes. A slight quiver shook his hand.

"Oh, Chief. What happened to you? Why are you here?"

A scratch of noise whispered from his mouth, his voice so quiet she wasn't even sure that he'd spoken. "Pardon me?"

His looked into her eyes and cleared his throat with one grunt. "Joseph." His voice cracked out the syllables of his name. How long had it been since he made any sound?

Her heart raced. "Nice to meet you, Joseph." She'd broken through. Now she had better back off before he scurried into the night, never to be seen again. "Can I leave you more sandwiches? You can have them later, maybe for dinner."

His head bobbed in a slight nod.

"Great. I'll leave you two." She looked behind her and then whispered. "Don't tell Angus." She winked and patted his shoulder then stood to leave. "I'll see you tomorrow, Joseph, okay?"

His eyes tracked her movements. Another slight nod.

On the way to her van she neared Angus and Frank who stood on the sidewalk. Angus winked and gave her thumbs up. "Jem," Frank whispered. "You ever think about changing jobs? You shrink heads real good."

"Well, I fixed you two, didn't I?"

Frank took one of her hands and kissed the back of it. "That you did, sweet lady. That you did."

nod and smile

Jem set her jaw and pressed the talk button. "Hello, Mother Wolfe."

Heavy breathing on the line. "Jemima."

"Althea, are you crying?"

"He's home. Thank you. Thank you for sending him."

Finn did that. "You're welcome. It's where he belongs, with you and his father."

"Yes, I agree. The funeral is a week from Saturday. At the Christ Church Cathedral on Burrard. Will you come?"

Would she come? Stupid woman. "I'll be there Friday night."

There was a long pause and then Althea cleared her phlegm-filled throat. "Do you want to stay here? Shall I prepare Gerald's old room for you?"

Jem's stomach churned. "I don't want to impose. You'll have so much going on. And I'm not sure I could handle that, in his room. I'll stay at the Georgia."

Althea *tsked* her. "A little out of your price range, don't you think?"

"I haven't been anywhere in four years. One night of luxury at one of the most difficult times in my life can't do me any harm."

"I suppose not. Perhaps that's best. My sister will be staying with me anyway so it may be a bit cramped."

Yes, two old ladies inside a twenty-eight-hundred-square-foot house would leave so little room for Jem. "What can I do? Do you need any help with the arrangements?"

"I'm sure I can handle this task on my own. Gerald's not the first man I've buried."

"I didn't mean to suggest you couldn't handle it. I'm only offering my support."

"You've done quite enough thank you."

The hair on Jem's neck stood on end. "I'm sorry? What does that mean?" It never failed. Any conversation with this woman on any topic, even the hardest topic of all time, ended up with Jem on the defensive and Althea on the attack.

"Do you think it's a coincidence that he got…. That his illness, if that's what it was, didn't start until he met you?"

Jem's right foot tapped the floor at a frenetic pace. Where the hell were her cigarettes?

"Again, Althea, paranoid schizophrenic. That was the diagnosis. You don't catch it like a cold. You aren't driven to it, and certainly not by someone who loves and supports you as much as I did him."

"Yes, support. With all those hours you worked helping other people, all those hours away from him."

"He worked as many hours as I did. More in fact. If anything, he didn't support me or my career." Her blood boiled. It was the same thing over and over, the same insane rants and complete ignorance of the facts. Of the clinical diagnosis. "The truth of it is that schizophrenia runs in the blood. It is a genetic disorder that is passed down from parent to child." Jem smirked. "Maybe you gave it to him."

A sharp intake of gravel breath scratched through the receiver. "How dare you? My family has no mental illness. None. And neither did Gerald."

Althea had an old fashioned phone. The crack of her slamming it a thousand miles away rung in Jem's ear.

Way to go Jemima. When will you learn to nod and smile?

it isn't cheating if he's dead

Jem jolted awake. The remnants of a bizarre dream of Gerald and Finn, both dressed in shining armour and jousting to win her love, flashed through her mind before disappearing in the dim night. She groped for the clock and pulled it towards her. Twelve-forty. She'd managed another twenty minutes of sleep.

She lay back down and rubbed her palms down her legs until they calmed under the duvet cover. She took a deep breath and closed her eyes. A moment later she was shocked out of temporary comfort by another restless leg jolt and a vision of Gerald's face slowly morphing into Joseph.

"What the hell?" She groaned and turned on her side, punched her pillow, and stuffed it under her neck. She shifted and twitched and bounced her head against the pillow again and again.

Enough of that crap.

She felt her way downstairs in the dark. By the glow of the under-counter lights she poured a full tumbler of wine, grabbed a chocolate chunk cookie from the pantry, and sank into the sofa. She turned on the television and scanned the program guide. Even with three hundred channels of digital cable there was nothing but shit on after midnight.

A thousand thoughts battled for attention in her muddled brain. Gerald's mangled body. Joseph's sunken cheeks and haunting stare.

Finn's lips on hers, the smell of his cologne and his sweat.

She found little more comfort than she had in her bed, still restless, her body twitchy. Her tank top shifted and bunched up around her braless breasts. She tugged it down and lay back.

Maybe she'd fall asleep right there in the living room. Numb her mind with reruns and bad shows. For the rest of her damn life.

There was a quiet knock at the door. She sat up fast. Blood rushed to her head. She hit the wine glass with one flailing hand and grabbed it before it tipped over. A few red drops hit the oak coffee table, like blood spatter on an alley floor.

At the entry, she flipped on the porch light. Finn's fine form was illuminated on the other side of the sheer curtain. The joy of the night before returned and hastened her heartbeat. She swung the inner door open and leered at him, one eyebrow raised. "You're six days early."

He pulled open the screen, swept her into his arms and consumed her in a ravenous kiss. Her feet didn't even touch the ground.

When he set her down and let go of her lips, he rested his forehead against hers. "Yeah. I think that weekly thing is out the window."

He picked her up and carried her up the stairs, her head resting on his shoulder. He hesitated on the last step.

He'd never been anywhere but the main floor in all these years. She nuzzled her nose into his neck and inhaled his cologne and the musk of his sweat. "Door on the left," she whispered in his ear.

He went left through the open door and laid her atop her overstuffed down quilt, still askew from her fitful attempts at sleep. With one knee on the bed and one foot on the floor he took off his suit jacket and hung it on the bedpost, loosened his tie and pulled it over his head. He stared at her while he unbuttoned his shirt.

She couldn't take her eyes off him. At the edge of her peripheral vision was a familiar frame. Its presence was a spectre observing her, witnessing her about to have sex with this beautiful man. It held a posed picture of her and Gerald. Their engagement picture taken a month before they bought the house. She was so young. So in love. So naïve.

She should turn it to face the wall. Shove it in a drawer. Hide it in the closet. But she didn't want to do anything to break the spell of that moment. Of Finn's consuming stare.

She should feel guilty. Feel some kind of remorse for having Finn in Gerald's bed. But she didn't. Was that terrible? Good thing she didn't believe in heaven or hell. She'd be damned for eternity if she did.

Her heart hammered, blood pulsated in her neck. She licked her lips and swallowed. Finn was muscle on lean muscle. Broad shoulders and trim waistline. Like no man she'd ever been with. The reality of him underneath his clothes was as good as her fantasies.

What the hell did he see in her? No, she would not question, would not self-deprecate. Not now.

He tossed his shirt on the floor, bent over her and planted tender, slow kisses from the fingertips of one arm up to her shoulder.

Shivers ran through her, goose bumps tingled over her entire body.

He lifted her tank top, licking and kissing her stomach and ribs, even her appendix scar, as he exposed her lily white flesh inch by inch. He glanced up at her and then slid her top over her breasts and peeled her shirt off. It joined his on the floor. With both hands, he ran his fingers from her collarbone to her nipples and down the sides of her torso.

Laughter caught in her throat. He smiled at her, then kissed, licked and sucked one nipple and then the other. Adrenaline burned in her abdomen and seared down her legs.

She pulled him closer and kissed him, pressing his chest to hers. She reached back, turned off the lamp beside the bed, and placed the picture face down on the table.

He reached over her and turned the lamp back on, bathing the bed in soft light. He smiled at her and flashed his eyebrows up and down.

She reached out and unbuckled his belt, then pulled his zipper down. He stood up and dropped his pants and boxers, kicking them aside. He tucked his fingertips into the waist of her yoga pants and slid them off.

"Going commando?"

She laughed. "I wasn't exactly expecting company." She pulled the bed sheet over her body.

He put one hand on her arm, wrested the sheet from her fingers and slid it away.

"Jem, what are you afraid of?"

She swallowed. "I'm not sure." She was afraid he'd see her. All of her.

He tossed her pants over his shoulder and dove onto the bed, landing with his elbows on either side of her. She anticipated her breath being knocked from her, but he rested delicately on top of her. Total control.

They kissed for minutes on end, his lips as strong as the rest of him, tongue hot in her mouth, his erection hard against her thigh.

He wrapped his arms around her and rolled onto his back, bringing her along for the ride.

She sat up and straddled his hips, lowering herself onto him. He reached up and caressed her breasts, ran his hands over her belly and down her thighs.

Her breath came in short puffs. She was so exposed and he was so scrutinous. What was he thinking? What did he see?

He pulled himself up, took her shins in his hands and wrapped her legs around his back. He kissed her neck and reached his arms under hers, held her shoulders with both hands.

She let go of her inhibitions and let her head drop back, closed her eyes and allowed herself to live in that moment.

His lips and tongue roamed the curves of her neck and chest. Then nothing but the cool air drying the trails of his saliva.

She opened her eyes to find him staring at her.

"Do you have any condoms? I think I'm going to burst."

Laughter shook her breasts. She pushed on his chest until he lay back down, reached across and opened the drawer on the night table. While she pulled a box from the drawer, he took one nipple in his mouth and rolled his tongue around it. She closed her eyes and swallowed. Warmth flooded her legs.

She pulled a packet from the box and tossed the box back in the drawer. He took it from her and eyed it.

"How old are these?"

"Well, to tell the truth." She grinned. "I bought them today."

"And you said you weren't expecting company." He ran one finger between her breasts, past her navel, and slid it between her legs.

She gasped and bit her lower lip. "You're one to talk mister rubber-in-the-wallet."

He grinned, licked his finger, ripped open the foil packet and handed her the condom.

She slid back, sat on his thighs and rolled it onto him.

He sat up to meet her, grabbed both of her butt cheeks and lifted her, bringing her back down on top of his erection. His body rocked and she undulated with him, his face buried in her neck.

She held his head and let him push her to the edge. But like the night before, he pulled away before she went over.

He shifted their bodies until he was lying behind her, her back and legs and ass all nestled against him. Then he found her again and filled her with gentle thrusts. He nibbled her neck and reached one hand around, pressing his fingers against her clitoris.

Her body spasmed and jerked. He held her tight and kept pressing, rubbing, fucking, kissing. She yelled out, unable to hold back her voice, unable to do anything but what her body insisted on doing, with or without her permission. Just when she didn't think she could take any more, he stiffened and groaned. Then he relaxed, pulled her into him and wrapped his legs around her.

She swallowed and blinked. "Wow."

He laughed. "Yeah. You could say that."

She turned in his arms and kissed him, staring into his eyes. It was like a dream. She was overwhelmed by the sudden realization that she'd been so lonely. So alone. For so long.

He kissed her forehead and slid from the bed, and stepped into the bathroom. He was back beside her in less than a minute, condom free. He pulled the covers over them. "I have to go soon. Got an early day."

"I understand." She didn't want him to leave.

She lay curled into the cocoon the intersection his arm and chest offered and ran her fingers along a line of fine hair from his belly button to the valley between his pecs. She slid her leg over his warm, powerful body, and became heavy with exhaustion.

"Ah, damn it."

She stirred awake at the sound of Finn's whispered curse. She lifted her head from his body. They must have been in the same position for hours. Rising sunlight streamed in the window and cut across his face.

"Is everything all right?"

He kissed her nose. "More than all right. Except I have to get to work." He squeezed her into him. "I'd rather stay with you."

She pushed herself to sitting and pulled the sheet over her body, aware of her naked form in the unforgiving morning light. She glanced over her shoulder. "You can use my shower. Save you some time." She scooted off the bed, pulled the sheet with her and wrapped it around her as she stood. In the mirror she saw him throw the quilt off and hop to his feet, unashamed of his naked body. What did that feel like, that confidence, that brazen love of yourself?

He stepped behind her and engulfed her in a hug, leaning over her shoulder to kiss her cheek. "Thanks, that would help. Not sure how to explain why I'm wearing the same suit two days in a row."

She leaned into his body and smiled. His erection against her butt took her breath from her. This man was a machine. "Tell them you got lucky."

"That I did."

"I'll go pour some coffee."

He spun her around, tugged the sheet from her hands and dropped it to the floor. He picked her up under her armpits and she wrapped her legs around his waist. He headed to the bathroom. "After a shower."

He sat her on the cold countertop and ran the water warm. She watched, trying to ignore her ever present self-consciousness. She avoided her reflection in the mirror and enjoyed the sight of him.

He took her hand and she jumped from the counter. They stepped into the bathtub and he held her close. He was hard against her. Pangs of arousal shot through her body. They made love right there, standing under the steamy heat of the shower.

They ran soap over each other's bodies and he shampooed her hair. Then they stood under the water and just held each other.

"Finn, why me?"

"Why you what?"

She pulled back and looked up at his face. "Why this? Why us?" She sighed. "Why me?"

"I don't understand what you mean."

"Look at you. You're a Greek god." She rested one palm on his chest and sighed. "I'm a little, shall we say, Rubenesque?"

One eyebrow shot up. "Rubenesque?"

"Yeah. You know. Fat."

"I know what it means, and you are not fat. You're not even Rubenesque. What you are is beautiful." He tightened his grip around her waist. His hand slid down to her wet ass and he squeezed. "Every ounce of you."

The heat rose in her cheeks. "Well I'm stacked. That's something."

His eyebrows furrowed. "You're lovely. Perfect auburn hair and golden eyes. High cheekbones and the dimple in your chin. That one snaggletooth." He ran his thumb over her bottom lip.

She searched his face for any sign of deception. Gerald had never told her she was beautiful. He didn't complain, but he was short on compliments.

Finn brushed the back of his fingers across her cheek. "But that's not why. It's because you are real. Honest. You are loyal and true. You waited for him, always kept hope. Four years is a long time."

She swallowed hard. "I don't feel so loyal right now."

"Jem, he's dead. You're not cheating on him. Not even on his memory. You respected him. Maybe more than he did you."

"I suppose that's true."

"It is true. I've been thinking about you — about us — for years. I've never met a woman like you. You love, truly and deeply

81

and without reservation. You care about everyone else more than you care about yourself."

All this time and she'd never noticed his interest. He was in total control of himself, never showed any emotion he didn't want her to see. But he never tried to control anything about her. Never belittled her opinion or questioned her choices.

She averted her gaze and looked at the shower curtain. "And I'm stacked."

"Yeah." He kissed the top of her head. "That too."

everyone has family

Finn stopped coming by for weekly nirvana updates. Instead he stopped in almost every day, at any hour. Whenever his messed up, always-on-call schedule would allow him enough time. Jem never said no. Some days he dropped by just to run his fingers through her hair and kiss her with a passion she was fast becoming accustomed to. Her favourite nights were when he slept in her bed until dawn.

They would make love at any hour. All hours. When they couldn't wait to be together, they dropped to the floor in the front entry and relished in the sweet release of raw sex. She had never initiated with Gerald. He was the in-control guy. But with Finn she was free. Free to go after what she wanted without fear of rejection. Without concern that he'd be uninterested, too busy, too tired. He was never any of those things. She felt more wanted in the past week than in all the years with Gerald combined. More beautiful. Hell, she felt beautiful for the first time in her life.

Finn surprised the hell out of her. Not how fast he flew into her bed — though after four years, could a month be considered fast? No, it was the truth of him. The real Finn she'd never seen before. Nothing like she expected. Not a 'just the facts ma'am' cop. Not all straight-spined, crisp-voiced, rugged and hard. This Finn was warm. Funny. Sexy as hell. His angles didn't seem so sharp any more.

She sat with Joseph every morning while he ate the food she

brought. He hadn't spoken again. He simply listened. And she took full advantage, releasing her sorrows on him. It helped her through her grief and seemed to break through small barriers with him.

Jem thought about Gerald less each day, her thoughts consumed instead by Finn. But when they discussed the case, her worlds collided. How ironic that her mind turned to her dead fiancé when her new lover was in the house.

Two days before Gerald's funeral, she finished packing sandwiches into the van when her cell phone rang. The number for Cecilia, Jem's legal assistant, flashed on the screen.

"Cece, you're working early."

"No shit. When the hell are you coming back? It's been, like, five weeks or something. I'm stuck here late, coming in early. And some of your clients are pissed. Richard says he's suing the firm if you don't start returning his calls."

"I'm doing okay, thanks for asking."

"Sorry, Jem."

"And Richard's contract is with the firm, not me. He can't sue."

"I know, but it doesn't stop him from calling me ten times a day."

Jem winced. "Sorry for that. But I'm just not ready yet. There's so much to process. I have to pack up all of Gerald's things. And I leave tomorrow morning for the funeral. Maybe after that I can get my shit together."

"Maybe. I hope so." Cecilia sighed into the receiver. "So, you been on a date yet?"

Jem smiled. Cece had tried to fix her up at least a dozen times. "Give me a break."

"Come on, girl. It's been four freaking years. When are you gonna get yourself some?"

"I'm hanging up now."

"What about that cop that's been calling you all the time? You said he was hot."

"Goodbye, Cece. I'll call you next week." Jem ended the call and smiled. Yes, he was hot all right.

"I won't be around for a couple of days." Jem peeled an orange, tore it in half and handed one piece to Joseph. "I wanted you to know. I've brought some peanut butter sandwiches. Not sure they'll last until Sunday but you can always go to the shelter. Maybe you should do that anyway. A nice shower, a hot meal. Even a real bed."

He shrugged.

"I'm going to Vancouver. Have to face Gerald's mother. Attend his funeral." She huffed. "I always figured we'd be married for decades and have a couple of grandkids before I had to do that. And of course, I'd be the one planning it, not his mother. I'd be his widow. His loving wife of forty-plus years. And his mother would be long-since dead." She pulled a section of orange off and popped it in her mouth. "It's funny how things turn out, eh? Never what you plan. Never how you dream it will be." She peeled another section and stared at her hands. "Oh shit, I'm sorry. That's your orange." She held it out for him.

He put his hand on her forearm, pushed it back to her and raised his eyebrows.

This was new, this sharing of food. She'd never done that with any other resident. "Thanks. I've got more in the van for you." She ate another section. Was it odd to consider a near-mute homeless man a friend when you only shared a one-sided conversation? He was her personal sounding board. A silent therapist. Maybe that was the best kind.

"I've talked your ear off about me, haven't I? What about you, Joseph?" She hesitated. "Can I call you Joe?"

85

He nodded.

"I don't know anything about you, Joe."

He stiffened, stopped eating the orange and stared at her.

"What about family? Everyone has family. Are your parents still alive?"

He shook his head with a sharp jerk.

"Oh. I'm sorry." She sat in silence for a few minutes and ate her half of the orange, one peeled section at a time. "Joe?"

He glanced up at her.

"Are you married?"

Another sharp shake of his head.

"But you wear a wedding band. I'm afraid it's going to fall off. You must have lost a lot of weight. Maybe you should move it to another finger."

He twirled the band on his ring finger and then made a fist. Another sharp shake of his head.

"All right. I understand." She glanced at Gerald's engagement ring on her own finger and twirled it.

She scanned the park. The residents went about their business, their wariness of Joe had waned and their interest in her interactions with him faded. She brought her attention back to him. "What about children, do you have kids?"

Silence. He hung his head and stared at the half-eaten orange in his lap. Then tears dripped onto it. His hands quaked and his shoulders shook.

"Oh, Joe." She scooted beside him and put her arms around him. He stiffened, didn't speak. Then his body melted under her touch. He leaned into her, his face against her shoulder, and sobbed.

She cooed at him like a mother to a distraught child and patted his head. She resisted the urge to wipe the grease from her palm.

What had happened to this poor man? And how could she ever

find out if he wouldn't tell her?

three men

"Call me if you need anything. Even just to vent." Finn stood at the departures gate, one hand cradling the side of Jem's face.

"I will. This is going to suck." She leaned her forehead against his chest and circled his waist with both arms. "Come with me?" she said into his breastbone.

"I would if I could. Honest." He lifted her face with one finger and laid a gentle kiss on her lips. "Only two days. Not even full days. I'll see you Saturday night."

She put her arms around his neck and kissed him, slowly and with tongue. Who cared who was watching? Public displays of affection were her new life's passion.

She sat in the window seat of the airplane and stared out at the mountain tops below. She ignored nature's beauty, her thoughts too crowded by the three men in her life.

Gerald, who for so long had been the only man she cared to think about, was front and centre today. Althea was devastated that the funeral couldn't be open casket. Too much damage from the beating he took, the autopsy, the fact he'd been dead more than a month, only frozen in the morgue, never embalmed.

Jem was relieved. She couldn't bear to look into his broken face. She would remember him at his prime, when he still had some small bit of fun and frivolity about him. When was that exactly? She shut her eyes and conjured the image of him that she loved best. 'It's getting hot in here. So take off all your clothes.' Yes, that was the Gerald she loved. The Gerald she would remember. The rest could melt away.

Visions of Finn pushed Gerald aside. Different kinds of thoughts, immediate memories. All wrapped around hammering heartbeats and knowing smiles and sluices of arousal-induced adrenaline. Finn was her future. Her present. Her gift.

And Joseph. Poor, poor Joe. He was the mystery. A mystery that baffled her even more than Gerald's disappearance and murder. Gerald's fate could be explained by his mental state. His insistence on stopping medication. It all came from that. How could anyone be surprised by the ending? Did she want the bastard that shot him caught? You bet. Did it consume her daily thoughts? Not anymore.

But Joe, he was always on her mind. Who was he? Where was his family? Someone must be looking for him. She had to find out.

The impact of the landing shook her from her thoughts.

First, she had to face Althea.

it runs in the blood

Jem sat at the window in her room at the Georgia Hotel and stared out into the courtyard below. Couples strolled towards the outdoor restaurant. The vibe of upbeat music seeped in through the windowpane. She rested her head against the glass and sighed. She'd rather be lounging on one of the teak couches next to the fire pit with Finn, sipping a Cosmo. Instead, she steeled herself for an evening with her no-longer-future mother-in-law.

Jem unpacked her funeral clothes and hung them to ease the wrinkles. Anything to avoid ironing. She checked her face in the mirror by the door, grabbed her purse, headed down to the lobby, and stepped out into the muggy air. The weather had turned on her. Another typical Vancouver day, overcast and raining. Bloody perfect.

"Taxi, miss?"

She nodded at the concierge in his crisp suit and cap. One wave of his hand and a cab pulled up. He opened the door for her. She pressed a five dollar bill into his hand and he tipped his hat.

On the doorstep of Gerald's old life she took two deep breaths and poked the doorbell. Westminster Quarters chimed from inside the house, a sound that always took her back to her grandfather's home when she was a child. She closed her eyes. The smell of aged newsprint and dusty books and the chimes of his antique mantle clock filled her head. Oh how she'd loved to sit in his library and touch every cover, open the pages and feel the history.

The door hinges squeaked. "Jemima? Why are you standing there with your eyes shut?"

Althea looked like hell. She'd lost at least twenty more pounds since their last meeting a year or so ago, the lines on her face had deepened and multiplied. Her ebony eyes were clouded like a frosted window into her frosty soul. A wave of sympathy surprised Jem. She searched her memory for one time, any time that she and Althea had gotten along. To a time when Althea wasn't an all out bitch. But nothing came to mind.

"Hello, Althea." Jem stepped forward and offered an awkward hug. She was met with a stiff response, a turned head, and one almost imperceptible pat on the back. As sentimental as always. The fact that Mother Wolfe never changed gave Jem an odd sense of comfort.

"Well come in already. Give me your jacket."

"Jemima, you beautiful girl. How are you handling all of this?"

Althea's sister, Marjorie, met her in the entry with a powerful long hug complete with rocking side to side. Marjorie was the polar opposite of her sister — and had always gotten along with Jem. She'd often fantasized that Marjorie was Gerald's real mother and that one day they'd let her in on some deep, dark family secret.

"I'm okay. I mean it's been four years. I was expecting the worst." It never failed. One hug from a sympathetic and caring individual, and an emotional flood ensued. She cried on Marjorie's shoulder.

"There, there." Marjorie's pudgy hand patted Jem's back. "You might think you were prepared, but how can you be, really?"

Althea's patented *tsk-tsk* cut her sorrow off cold. "All right, enough of that. Go sit in the living room, I'll bring tea."

"Do you have wine?" Jem pulled away from Marjorie's embrace, smiled at her and winked. "I'd rather have a drink."

Althea gave her a cold look. "I suppose. If you must."

Marjorie put her arm around Jem's shoulder. "We must. Red, right hon?"

Jem nodded. "Red."

They set off to the living room. Althea shuffled away towards the kitchen. Two glasses of wine later the door chimes announced the arrival of other mourners. There would be no viewing and for that, Jem was thankful. Instead Althea insisted people drop by and share their memories of her beloved son.

Doctor Lewis stepped across the threshold. Jem hadn't seen Gerald's psychiatrist since not long after his disappearance. What was the point? There was no one to treat. But Althea had been in constant contact. Jem was baffled by this. The woman refused to believe her son was mentally ill, but she was relentless in her hounding of this poor man. How on earth could he help find Gerald?

When the doctor caught sight of Jem, he nodded and waved, then made his way to her side of the room.

"Jem, dear. How are you holding up?"

"I'm fine Sid. Really, I am."

"I guess four years eases some of the loss, eh?"

She nodded and sipped her wine. No, it didn't ease it. If anything, it made it more profound. Having Finn made it less difficult. But no one here could know that. Althea would have her head.

Within an hour, the small front room was crowded with Marjorie's adult children, their spouses and their many offspring. The kids, too young to understand what the meeting represented, some of them born after Gerald's disappearance and none of them able to remember him at all, ran around and laughed and screeched. Althea ran around after them, snatching precious objects from their curious hands, moving crystal tumblers and blown-glass elephants and a multitude of framed snapshots from arms reach. There were no toys to keep a child occupied in Althea's grandchild-barren home. The blame for that rested its full weight on Jem's shoulders.

Jem sat in an antique wing chair in the corner and shifted against the unyielding upholstered seat. She watched the kids run. Her heart was lightened by their smiling faces, the ease with which they laughed.

What would her and Finn's children be like? Their daughter would be statuesque and lean, but curvy like her mother. Their son would be tall and strong, handsome as his father. They'd both be brilliant and beautiful and kind and honest. They would have the best of both parents.

The noise in the room shook her from her thoughts and her cheeks warmed. Where did that come from? The idea of having Finn's babies. Befitting little fantasy to have at Gerald's mother's house on the eve of his funeral.

Hours later, when most of the mourners had vacated the house, Jem sat on the sofa with Marjorie. Althea and Doctor Lewis stood near the mantle. With one too many merlots fuelling her confidence, Jem was in the mood to push her luck.

"Sid, was it you who told me schizophrenia is genetic? It runs in the blood?"

Althea's stare bore into her.

Doctor Lewis cleared his throat and loosened his tie. "Well, yes, yes I guess I did." Sweat beaded on his brow. He stole a glance at Althea and then took a gulp of gin and tonic. "Several genes are implicated in schizophrenia. There are new studies that show that it's not entirely genetic though."

Althea crossed her arms and smirked. "There you go Jemima. I told you he didn't get it from my family."

Did she just admit he had it at all?

"Although." Sid turned to Althea. "People with first-degree relatives who carry the gene or have the disease are much more susceptible."

"What does that mean, 'first-degree?'" Althea paced.

"It means it's more likely that a schizophrenic has one or more schizophrenic parents than has an aunt or a cousin who is schizophrenic. And the incidence of the disease in people with no genetic history is quite small. So if we were betting folk, we could place money that someone else in Gerald's close family has the disease."

Jem nodded. "Or carries the gene."

"Yes. Or that."

"Bullshit."

"Althea!" Marjorie gaped at her sister.

"Gerald wasn't ill. Was not schizophrenic. I'll believe that until the day I die."

"Mrs. Wolfe, please." Doctor Lewis pulled a handkerchief from his jacket pocket and wiped his brow. "We've been over this a hundred times. The diagnosis was sound. Gerald improved with medication. If he'd stayed on it, things might have turned out differently. He could have coped, could have managed. Could have even continued his research."

Althea dropped into the brocade wing chair, her shoulders slumped. "Bullshit," she said under her breath.

"Maybe it runs in his father's family?" Jem looked at Althea. "Did your husband show any signs?"

Althea stood and glared at her. "Damn you, Jemima, why must you push this? What does it matter now? Gerald's father is dead. Gerald is dead. You never got around to giving me grandchildren. Even if any of it was true, and it's not, there's no one left to pass it down to. No one left to lose their goddamn mind." She went to the front door and opened it. "Time for you to go. I need to sleep if I'm to survive tomorrow." She headed for the stairs. "Show yourselves out."

The ticking of the grandfather clock echoed in the silent room. Jem ran a finger around the rim of her wine glass. What the hell was wrong with her? Maybe Althea was right, maybe it didn't matter. She had to get over this incessant need to push Althea's buttons and make her face the truth. Althea's own truth wasn't many years away. More like months.

"Well, I should be going." Doctor Lewis pulled his tie off, shoved it in his pocket and turned to Jem. "I'll see you tomorrow. Maybe we shouldn't speak of Gerald's disease any longer. It'd be for the best."

"Yes, of course. I'm sorry Sid. I don't know what came over me."

"Sure you do." Marjorie poured Jem another glass of wine. "My sister's had a hate-on for you since the first time Gerald brought you home. I never understood why, I think you're a treat. But you two were made to pour salt in each other's wounds." She patted Jem on the shoulder. "Don't you worry about it. You had a right to know. Especially before he died." She sighed. "But she's right, you know. It doesn't matter now."

"It matters to me." Jem wiped tears from her cheeks with the back of her hand. "Maybe if I knew, I could find an answer to all the whys. Why did he go off his meds? Why did he leave?" She hung her head. "Why did he prefer crazy with strangers to some semblance of normal life with me?" She looked at Marjorie. "If he didn't want me, he could have said so. So it does matter to me. If I could even begin to understand why, then I might be able to close the Gerald door. Move on. Start over. There's a new door waiting to be opened."

Doctor Lewis shifted his weight from foot to foot. "Maybe we can talk when we get back to Calgary. I'll give you a call and come by the house. With Gerald gone, I think the doctor-patient privilege rules don't need to be so strictly enforced."

Jem's heart sped up. Sid knew why Gerald was ill. All this time?

Marjorie walked the doctor to the door and closed it behind him. She turned to Jem. "Now. I want to hear all about the man behind door number two."

"Oh Marj. I need a cigarette."

"Oooh, me too. Let's go sit on the porch."

one of the unfaithful

The ringing phone jarred Jem awake. She sat up too fast. Pain stabbed her temples. She snatched the receiver.

"This is your nine-thirty wake-up call."

Nothing like a robotic pre-recorded message to shock you into a nasty wine hangover. She should have passed on those last couple of glasses but Marjorie was hard to say no to.

When the cab dropped her off at the hotel the night before, she found herself wide awake. She called Finn and, for the first time in her life, had phone sex. They went from filling each other in on their days to her railing on about Althea to detailed descriptions of what they were doing to themselves while masturbating a thousand kilometers apart. When she hung up the phone she felt satisfied, uncomfortable, and just plain silly. But Finn didn't mind it one bit. Even at a distance, in the middle of the night, awakened from a dead sleep by her phone call, he wanted her. She'd fallen asleep at four o'clock hugging the extra pillow and dreaming of him.

She swung her legs over the side of the bed and ran her hands through her hair. She poked at the phone and made a quick call to room service before she jumped into a steaming shower.

Minutes later, enveloped in a thick hotel robe with a towel wrapped around her wet hair, she answered a quiet knock at her door. A young fellow in a maroon waistcoat and starched white shirt whirled into the room, a tray balanced on one hand. She salivated at the smell that wafted from the hole in the chrome plate cover.

She signed the chit, tipped him twenty-five percent, and showed him out. The best hangover cure ever — greasy food and strong coffee. She sat at the table by the window and gobbled two eggs over medium, maple sausage, and buttery toast while she scanned the view. With only one crust of bread remaining on her plate, she guzzled her coffee and glanced at her watch. "Shit." Time to face the funeral music. And Althea.

She did her hair up, clipping and spraying it into place. She put on makeup, something rare for her, saved for special events and court appearances. A little lip gloss to bring out her natural pout, a touch of eye shadow and mascara. Despite a full night of hanging in the closet, her suit was still wrinkled — the black jacket, grey pencil skirt, even the lavender silk blouse.

Damn it. Ironing after all.

Once dressed, she slipped on her highest heels, the lavender patent-leather ones with the peep toe that revealed her lacquered nails, an indulgence she rarely bothered with. She poked pearl studs through her pierced ears, stood in the front entry, and analyzed her reflection in the mirrored closet doors.

"Wow. Not bad, old girl." Normally her curves screamed 'fat girl' at her, but today she saw beauty looking back. A woman who'd seen her share of the crap in the world. Who'd come out, stronger and happier, on the other side. How strange, to realize that on this day. She still didn't have many answers. Still didn't know why Gerald made the choices he did. But they were his choices. Not hers. Maybe after today she could let some of it go. Get on with her life. A life without Gerald. And blessedly, without Althea either.

She pulled her cigarettes from her purse and tapped on the pack. Nothing. She shook it. Empty. She tossed the pack in the garbage can. A day without vices. No smokes. No wine. And no Finn.

Her belongings packed, she checked out of the hotel and left her bags with the concierge. There'd be enough time after the service and obligatory showing for tea and finger sandwiches afterward to stop back for them on her way to the airport. But not enough time to change. Wait until Finn got a load of this outfit.

She stepped out onto West Georgia Street into a sparkling morning. The ever-present odour of salt water and fish wafted from Vancouver Harbour a few blocks away. She'd always hated that smell.

Twelve-thirty. What a ridiculous time for a funeral. But knowing Althea, it was her way to guarantee as many people as possible would come back after the interment. Bring 'em in hungry with the promise of food. Then the grieving mother would soak up all the sympathy she could.

Even the location was so wrong. A church. Gerald hadn't stepped inside a church since he was ten. He'd already finished high school and was on his way to university before he hit fifteen. He was brilliant, a genius. The idea of a higher power simply amused him. No matter how much his mother tried to convince him otherwise, he wouldn't attend. He scoffed at her beliefs, but he never told Althea that. Jem was glad her parents didn't have religion. Made being an atheist so much easier.

She could have argued with Althea, about the church, about the burial. But what was the point? Jem wouldn't have been heard. And she no longer gave a shit. If Gerald wanted to roll over in his grave, so be it. It's his own damn fault he'll be in one to begin with. He should have discussed his wishes with his mother, not with her. He knew Althea would never listen, never give in. But maybe he didn't think Althea would live long enough to see his funeral. Maybe by the time he left, all that didn't matter anymore. Maybe he just wanted to be gone.

Two blocks up and one right turn later she stood in front of the cathedral. Belief or no belief, Jem couldn't help but admire the old church, its architecture and sandstone exterior, the Gothic arch stained-glass windows. She mounted the stairs, hesitating on each step. She stopped halfway to take it all in.

The Heritage Horns at Canada Place belted out the first four notes of O Canada. She glanced at her watch. Noon on the dot. Seven-and-a-half hours until she'd be thousands of feet in the air, leaving all of this behind her. For good. Less than nine until Finn would meet her at the airport and gather her in his arms. Another hour after that and she would be pushed to the brink of ecstasy over and over again until plunging into the sexual abyss with him. Had sex ever been this good before?

The sign above the church door caught her attention. Alleluia indeed.

She stepped inside the vestibule behind a dozen others waiting to be shown a seat. A dozen perfumes clashed and fought to be noticed amid the overpowering aroma of lemon furniture polish and aged dust.

A guest book sat to the right of the doorway to the main hall of the church. She signed it and added 'You will be with me forever.' She ran one finger down the list of names already waiting inside. Dean was there with his wife. She would seek them out, sit in friendly territory.

An usher took her by the elbow and led her into the cavernous space. She was overcome by the beauty of the wood and the fixtures and the height and breadth of the room. Her gaze focused upward until a polite tug on her elbow stopped her short in the aisle. She bumped into a man in front of her.

"My apologies," she murmured.

"Jem, come with me." Marjorie took over for the usher and

tucked an arm inside of hers, clasping hands. "As you might expect, Althea's in fine form this morning. I know your concerns, I understand your right to know answers. But maybe today you could let it go and just be here for her, okay?"

"Don't worry. I have no desire for a scene in the middle of Gerald's funeral. I'll go sit with Dean." She scanned the heads in the pews.

"Don't be silly. You belong up front with the family." Marjorie put an arm around her waist and guided her forward. "I mean really," she leaned her head next to Jem's, "you were more family than most of us. You knew him best."

And with that, Jem burst into tears. Marjorie pulled a Kleenex from the pocket of her sweater and handed it to her then slid into the front pew. Jem followed, Marjorie and her family creating a blockade between Jem and Althea. The woman didn't even glance up at her, no reassuring smile, not even a nod. But what did she expect? That on the day of his funeral Althea would come around and see that Jem loved him, after all these years of assuming the worst?

Maybe Althea was right about her. The man she'd loved, searched for, waited for, lost —he'd been dead only a few weeks and her head was already filled with thoughts of another. Thoughts she couldn't control, not even in Gerald's mother's home. Not even on the threshold of an inappropriate church funeral meant to honour the memory of the brilliant scientist, atheist, corduroy-loving man she held out hope would come home to her.

She should change her name to Jezebel.

Gerald lay a few feet from her. His coffin, a white brocade cloth with gold bands forming a cross lain over it, rested front and centre for all to see. He was right there. In the room. Close enough to touch. For the first time in years.

She squeezed her eyes shut and conjured his face but details

101

refused to appear. Wisps of him came to mind. Small pieces of memory. A lock of hair, a flash of ebony eye. Tears streamed down her cheeks. He'd lost his mind, but she'd lost his whole body, and now he was starting to fade altogether.

She dabbed at her eyes with the tissue and stared up at the stained glass. Five sections, each Gothic arch larger than the last, working from the outsides in. The centre arch, a good twenty feet tall, towered over the faithful in the pews. And one of the unfaithful.

The portrayals were detailed with beautiful colours, vibrant and glowing, backlit by the bright sun that chose to bathe this rainy city in light on this day, of all days. The only figure she recognized was Jesus. What was that he stood on, an ice floe? No, a cloud. Of course. An ice floe would make more sense though, help to explain the whole walking on water thing.

In the centre pane, he spread his arms, his haloed head proof that this scene took place after the resurrection. He addressed the huddled masses below him. It looked more like cowering than huddling. Bowing at the feet of someone his disciples aspired to be. Someone they never could be. Someone they loved without reservation. Someone they were afraid of losing again.

The room filled with the sound of shuffling feet and clearing throats and nervous coughs. Her watch announced it was twelve-oh-five. Time to get this show on the road.

As if summoned, the minister entered from a side door and stood next to Gerald's coffin. Women lawyers were a sin against nature, but Althea attended a church with a female minister. Did that make her a hypocrite, or maybe a little enlightened? Perhaps Jem was the only woman mother Wolfe had total disdain for.

The minister placed her hand on the cloth and looked out at the congregation.

"We meet in the name of Jesus Christ, who died and was raised to the glory of God the Father. Grace and mercy be with you." The minister cleared her throat. "We have come here today to remember before God our brother Gerald. To give thanks for his life. To commend him to God our merciful redeemer and judge. To commit his body to be buried, and to comfort one another in our grief."

Over the next hour the congregation was asked to rise, to sing, to pray, to sit. Jem rose and sat, but singing and praying were out of the question. She stood, but never bowed her head, never uttered the words of a God she did not believe in. A God that didn't exist at all. Whose words were those, anyway? Some ancient storyteller perhaps. The original novelist.

When the minister began the eulogy, Jem snapped out of her contemptuous thoughts and paid attention. This woman that Gerald had never met was telling the story of him. The story his mother wanted told. Why wouldn't Althea allow her to speak? To share her Gerald with this crowd of mostly strangers and acquaintances. They were regaled with tales of Gerald the perfect son, Gerald the precocious genius, Gerald the brilliant scientist. Predictions that, had he lived, he would have cured all cancers for good.

Where was the Gerald who alphabetized the soup? How about the Gerald who stripped to hip hop music and fucked her on the couch? The Gerald who listened to the others and spoke to them through the pearl in her ring. The Gerald who lost his freaking mind. Where was he? He'd been swept under the communion carpet, never to be spoken of again. If sticking your head in the sand were a sin, Althea would rot in hell.

The minister stood by the coffin. "Please, I welcome you to join me and gather around Brother Gerald."

No one moved. Jem stole a look at Althea, then stood and smoothed the front of her skirt. Murmurs filled the hall. She joined the minister at Gerald's side and placed a hand on the coffin. With one touch of her living flesh to the container that held his cold body, grief overcame her and she wept.

The shuffling of many feet was followed by several people gathering around the coffin. Marjorie was on one side of her. Dean slid next to the other, put his arm around her waist and kissed her cheek. Althea remained seated, her head in her hands, her shoulders quaking.

"Let us commend Gerald to the mercy of God, our maker and redeemer. Please bow your heads in silence."

Jem bowed her head, but not in prayer. In silence for Gerald. Something he sought for so long. Silence in his head.

"And now to he who is able to keep us from falling, and lift us from the dark valley of despair to the bright mountain of hope, from the midnight of desperation to the daybreak of joy."

From despair to hope. Desperation to joy. If only that were possible, for Gerald's sake.

"To him be power and authority, forever and ever."

"Amen."

The chorus of voices around her, loud and sudden, shook her to the core like a twenty-one gun salute.

Everyone returned to the pews and took their seats. The minister invited the pall-bearers to flank the casket. Dean, Marjorie's two sons, and three men Jem had never met grasped the brass handles and rolled Gerald up the aisle. Jem was the first one to exit behind him. She walked up the aisle alone. The only aisle she would ever walk with Gerald. Like a morbid reverse wedding.

Row by row the pews emptied and mourners fell in behind her, all hushed murmurs and muffled sobs. Outside the church, the pallbearers hoisted the casket and carried it down the many steps. Jem stood on the sidewalk, unable to look away from the coffin. When they slid it into the open maw at the rear of the hearse, her heart sank. She'd known he was dead. That he wasn't coming home. Had even started to move on. But the vision of that vehicle swallowing him whole made it final. Made it stick. Made him gone forever.

The hearse door slammed shut. She flinched, closed her eyes, and hung her head.

"Jem?" Marjorie touched her arm. "We've got the limo. You come with us."

"No. I can't. I can't watch her stuff him into a hole in the cold ground. None of this is what he would have wanted."

"I understand." Marjorie hugged her, pinning her arms to her sides. "Althea won't, but that's not important now," she whispered. "You have to do what is right for you." She stood back and gripped both Jem's arms. "Will you wait here? Have lunch and tea?"

"Of course."

Marjorie climbed into the limo and it pulled away from the curb, following behind the hearse. A line of cars fell into its wake, idling down Burrard Street and heading to Mountain View Cemetery. Jem watched the procession until the last carful of mourners turned right on Dunsmuir.

She slipped off her shoes, slid her fingers through the peep toes, and walked in the opposite direction, stilettos bouncing off her thigh. Her mind was bombarded with flashes of the past nine years. No, not the full nine. Only the five years before he disappeared.

She ran every moment of passion, every not-crazy Gerald time they shared, through a mental projector. She remembered each one in detail, what he wore, what he said, how he smelled. Those occasions weren't especially memorable, but they were rare. His real passion was reserved for his research, for his life's goal. She was an afterthought. Always had been. She just didn't realize it until he was gone.

Was that why she held on so tight to hip hop sex and ass slapping moments? Had she replayed them so often they'd become the legend of their relationship? The fantasy that was her version of Gerald — not the reality. Those moments weren't him, only small bits of him. The best bits that he meted out in tiny doses. He didn't withhold them on purpose. It was who he was. He didn't know any better. Didn't know how to not be a genius, not be gifted.

When he started to dip his toe into mental illness, all the signs were there. She saw them. But she misinterpreted them, didn't recognize them for precursors to schizophrenia. No, she thought they were signs he was learning to relax. Learning to be silly and enjoy life's goofy moments. With her.

But that wasn't what happened. It was his brain on schizophrenia. The early symptoms of the greater problems to come.

In the years before the mental break, the Jem that used to be disappeared into the Gerald that was. Her ideals and career became secondary to his. He never understood why she spent her time defending criminals and hoodlums. No matter how she explained he didn't listen. It wasn't a higher calling like his. Wouldn't save millions of lives, even though he only wanted to save one. He was more like his mother than she'd ever realized.

Why did he love her? Maybe he never did. Maybe his love for her was a reflection of her adoration of him.

Maybe it was time to rediscover who she used to be.

Finn's face took over her thoughts and she smiled. She was coming back. He was bringing her back. But he didn't even know it.

Perhaps she should give herself more credit. She was bringing herself back. Back into life. With him as the incentive to rejoin the bigger world. To leave all the Gerald stuff behind.

Forty minutes later she found herself at the entrance to the Georgia Hotel, her feet aching and filthy. She ducked into the lobby bathroom and washed them before sliding back into her shoes. It was harder this time, her feet swollen from the high heels and the walk. Maybe she should pull her sneakers out of her luggage. No, Finn had to see her like this, at least once.

She collected her overnight bag from the concierge, pulled up the handle and rolled the bag behind her. The wheels clacked against the lines in the sidewalk. At the church, the vestibule was empty. The church was empty. Where was everyone? She wandered the halls until the minister came out from behind a door.

"Are you looking for the Wolfe reception?"

"Yes, thank you. I guess I got turned around."

"We've just come back from the interment. Go around the corner here and it's the second door on your left."

Jem stepped around the corner. A crowd neared from the other direction. She'd made one wrong turn and ended up full circle, almost to where she'd started.

She stepped into the room and headed to a far corner. Tables butted up against each other made a long buffet in the middle of the mourners. A cacophony of voices and laughter and slurping and chewing assaulted her. How soon could she escape and return to the safety of her little aging two-story home?

She tucked her bag behind a row of chairs and turned to find Althea right behind her.

"Jemima, I'm sorry you felt you couldn't come to the interment." Her crossed arms shielded her from any potential hug Jem might offer. Had they ever hugged before yesterday?

"We all grieve in our own way. That would have been a bit too much to witness. Did it go well? Were you pleased with this celebration of Gerald?"

Althea softened, her shoulders relaxed and her arms fell to her sides. "Yes." Tears sprung from her eyes. "It was almost perfect."

Jem wasn't going to ask what 'almost' meant. Instead she set aside their differences, if even for that brief moment. A mother who'd lost her only child stood in front of her. A mother in pain. She put her arms around Althea's frail frame and hugged her. "I'm so sorry, Althea. So very sorry."

Her hug was not returned, but Althea's head rested on her shoulder. The clips in her hair poked Jem through her suit.

"Thank you, Jemima." Althea recoiled and straightened as if she realized she'd slept with the enemy. "Go ahead and have some tea. Maybe a sandwich or two. There are some low-fat options. Maybe steer clear of the dessert trays."

Ten seconds. The full length of their truce and shared moment of grief. And she survived it with only one sideswipe at her weight.

Althea moved through the crowd. Warm hugs and sympathetic coos were heaped upon her. Jem stood alone.

She'd never known any of the family but Marjorie. Never met any of the family friends. When Gerald went home to visit, she usually stayed in Calgary, too busy with cases to get away. Too happy to avoid his mother's constant barbs. He never noticed them. It was always Jem that overreacted, misunderstood, read things into his mother's words. He was blind to Althea's poison.

An arm slid around her waist and a dry kiss graced her cheek.

"How you doing, hon?" Dean's wife, Anna squeezed her ribs. "About ready to bolt?"

"You got it." She reached out and took Dean's hand, then accepted a warm hug. Gerald's partner couldn't have been more different than Gerald. Suit pressed and starched, double Windsor at the Adam's apple, hair trimmed close around his ears and held in place with some kind of greasy product. Not funeral wear for Dean. It was his daily uniform.

Jem struggled to make small talk or even care how he was doing.

"Dean, did Gerald ever tell you about his dad? He only ever told me about the heart attack. What was he, thirty-four?"

"That's what I understand."

"My dad died the same way. At forty-two. I always thought that was too young for heart problems, but thirty-four? Seems unreal."

Dean tucked his hands in the front pocket of his pants and rocked on his heels. "Yeah. Unlikely. But I guess it could happen. I mean it's not unheard of."

"Sounds like you don't believe it."

He sighed. "When Gerald started to… you know. Lose it." He smoothed the sides of his hair and rubbed his hands. "Look, he never wanted you to know. But his dad didn't have a heart attack."

Her focus narrowed, the only thing in her vision was Dean's face which was crimson. Sweat beaded on his forehead. She grit her teeth. "What do you mean?"

Anna placed a gentle hand on her husband's arm. "Darling, this isn't the time nor place."

Marjorie popped her head over Dean's shoulder. "How you all doing? Can I get tea or a lemon square for anyone?"

"Marjorie." Jem's teeth were clenched, her body stiff. "How did Gerald's father die?"

Marjorie looked sideways at Dean and then scanned the room. "Jem, can we discuss that another day? You promised, nothing upsetting today."

"Well, I'm pretty upset. To learn that for nine years I've been told a lie. Believed it. The only reason to lie about it is because the truth is too terrible to tell."

"What is too terrible to tell?"

Jem spun around to find Althea right behind her, arms crossed and fists clenched.

"How your husband really died. It wasn't a heart attack, so what did happen, Althea?"

"Jem, please." Marjorie gripped her arm and tugged her away but Jem stood in place and yanked her arm free.

Althea tapped one sensible shoe against the short pile carpet. "A heart attack stole him from us far too soon. He was a wonderful man, Jemima, a wonderful father and husband. How dare you question that?"

"I'm not questioning that. I never questioned anything about him until today. Until I learned that your son knew he didn't die of a heart attack but never told me the truth. Why?"

"Maybe it's time you went home. You don't belong here. You never did."

Marjorie stepped between them. "Althea, stop. She's lost the love of her life, you've got to realize that. She's grieving too. We all are. You are not the only one in pain, not the only one who loved him. And you are not the only one that he loved." She took her sister's hand. "Jem has a right to know."

Althea pulled away. "Not from me she doesn't." She walked away.

One door of Jem's life slammed shut at that moment. She'd never have to deal with Gerald's mother again. Hooray for small mercies. She looked from Anna to Dean to Marjorie. "So? Who's spilling the beans?"

"Not here." Dean looked at his watch. "Do you have time for a coffee before your flight?"

good enough to eat

Jem dragged her overnight bag behind her. A blister on the back of her left heel rubbed against the inside of her beautiful, torturous shoe. She almost couldn't squeeze her feet back into them when the flight landed. Almost didn't want to.

So much for making an entrance. Shoulders slumped, exhausted by grief and lies, and a blister limp. She'd give Quasimodo a run for his money.

She stepped through the exit doors and into meeting place D. Finn leaned against a column, the overhead lights illuminating him like a beacon. He scanned the crowd. When his eyes caught hers, her heart soared. It took all of her self-control not to break into a run and jump into his arms. Instead she smiled and waved and picked up the pace, her stilettos click-click-clicking on the marble floor.

Finn pushed himself off the column with his shoulder. When he broke into a jog, she threw self-control out the window and ran to him. She dropped her luggage and jumped into his arms. He caught her, held her against him and kissed her with no regard for what anyone watching might think. It was the most romantic moment of her life.

"Are you up for dinner?" He set her down and brushed her hair from her face.

"Haven't you eaten?"

"I had a late lunch." He ran his hands down her back and rested them on her butt. "I'd like to skip ahead to dessert. You look good enough to eat." He flashed his eyebrows at her. His tie was loosened, his crisp white shirt unbuttoned to below his collarbone. Maybe she was having a positive effect on him too.

"I can get on board with that idea. Dessert." She ran one finger from his chin to the opening of his shirt. "And wine. I am in desperate need of both."

He pushed the handle of her luggage down, picked up the bag and took her hand. They headed for the exit and he leaned his head towards her. "You can tell me all about the funeral."

"Oh, that's a mood killer. Let's save that for nirvana. Tomorrow, okay? I've got lots to tell you, but I need to get some distance from it first. Some perspective."

"Uh oh. Pretty bad?"

"Pretty surprising. And yet, not at all. On the plus side, I doubt I'll ever hear from Althea again. I knew she didn't like me. But now I'm sure she hates me."

"You rabble-rouser."

"Damn straight."

keep the uglies away

The cell phone vibrated against the wood of the nightstand, followed by one gentle chime. Jem stuck her hand out and fumbled along the edge, her eyes shut against the rising sun. When the phone was in her grip, she squinted one eye open. Four-fifty-nine in the morning. One text waiting. From Finn.

She stacked her pillows behind her and sat up. The alarm clock agreed, four-fifty-nine. He was punctual, her love machine. She turned the alarm off and looked at the small screen of her phone.

'Good morning.'

She grinned and thumbed her keyboard. 'Good morning to you. Wish you could have stayed longer.'

'Sorry. Some partiers found a body floating in the Bow River.'

'Gross.'

'Nirvana tonight?'

'Yes. Come for dinner?'

'I can be there about eight.'

'Can't wait. I'm going to buy a barbecue.'

'Tofu burgers?'

Not anymore. 'T-bones.'

'Aren't you a vegetarian?'

'That was Gerald's thing. I did it for him.'

'Isn't it better for you?'

'Screw that. I want meat. You know, the cow kind.' She added a winky face.

'We can arrange for more than one helping of meat.' It was followed by a heart.

A heart. Was that a declaration of love? On a text? No, don't over think it. Go with the flow and enjoy the ride.

'Three or four, perhaps?'

'As much as you wish.'

'Excellent. See you later.' Her thumb hesitated over the send button. She threw caution to the wind and added a heart. Send.

She bounced out of bed and jumped into the shower. A pop song hummed from her lips. She hadn't just met him, and maybe this was crazy. But it was a good kind of crazy. The only kind of crazy she ever wanted in her house again.

An hour-and-a-half later, boxes of sandwiches and drinks and fruit rested on the floor of the van. She made her way to the park and slid into the same familiar parking spot, searching the periphery of the bushes. Her heart fell. No Joe in the shrub. She scanned the park but he was not in sight. Frank and Angus were asleep under their tree like most of the residents. She was a half-hour early.

She sipped sweet coffee from her travel mug, her heart in her throat, eyes darting all directions in search of Joe. Had she pushed too hard? Did he bolt to get away from her incessant nosiness? Or maybe he was like Gerald — holding onto a deep, dark, family secret that drove him to where he is now. Pushed him over the edge and kept him away from those who loved him.

When more people started to stir and Angus stretched and sat up, she exited the van and slid open the cargo door. She tossed boxes of food into the wagon and rushed to the sidewalk. A middle-aged woman with pink and purple bows clipped to her gray dreadlocks helped Jem pull the wagon over the curb.

"Thanks, Flossie. Here, take an extra juice box."

Flossie's eyes lit up. "You're a dear."

Following her usual path, she distributed sandwiches starting at the near end of the park and working her way to the far end. Where Joe should be. She made small talk with the residents, but didn't ask questions, didn't probe like usual.

When she approached the elm, Angus nudged Frank with his foot. "Wake up man. Ruby's here."

Frank rolled over and shaded his eyes from the morning. "Hey, you're back." He sat up. "How was the funeral?"

"It was fine." Liar. "Where's Joe?"

"Isn't he back?" Angus craned his neck and searched the line of bushes. "Well shit, we figured he went for a walk."

"A walk?"

"Yeah." Frank scratched his beard. "Got up yesterday afternoon and wandered off."

"In the daytime? He usually only moves under the cover of night."

"I know, right? He even waved at us a little."

"A couple of new dudes came by and were eyeing his spot." Angus pointed to where Joe should be sitting. "But me and Frankie, we told 'em to beat it. To find a new squat. That one was reserved for Chief."

"That was nice of you. He's kind of grown on you, hasn't he?"

"Yeah. Like a tacky vase or something."

Frank laughed. "Truth is he kind of keeps watch. Keeps the uglies away. You know, not by chasing anybody or anything. Or even yelling. Just by being freaky looking. Gonna miss that crazy son of a bitch."

"Maybe he'll be back." Jem tapped her thighs with both hands.

He had to come back. She'd gotten through to him. Gotten into

115

his head. Or maybe he'd gotten into hers.

three helpings of meat

"Jem?"

Finn's voice echoed through the house and met her on the patio. "I'm out back."

She held the instruction book for her new charcoal grill in one hand, a long match in the other. A cone of briquettes had been soaked in lighter fluid and she counted to thirty in her head. She lit the match, stood back, reached in and lit the coals at the bottom. The initial stink of burning fuel caught in her nostrils and overpowered the perfume of the neighbour's blooming lilac bush. She circled around to the other side of the grill and lit another spot.

Finn filled the frame of the sliding French door. "You left your front door open. Anybody could have come in."

"Yeah, sorry. I can't hear the bell out here."

"Wow, you got an old-fashioned one."

"I did indeed. Haven't lit one in so long I forgot how." She dropped the match into the grill and tossed the book onto the frosted glass tabletop. "They make things taste better than propane. More barbecuey."

He skipped down the wooden stairs, his feet bare, tie already gone. He stood in front of her and kissed her forehead. "Is that a real word?"

"You bet it is." She grabbed both his ass cheeks and pulled him against her, then kissed him while the smell of burning charcoal filled the yard.

The scrape of a door sliding in its frame and the clomping of feet on her neighbour's deck made her pull away. She looked over the short fence to find old Mr. Rowbotham gawking at them.

She waved. "Hi Ed. Nice night for a barbecue."

Ed lifted his teacup in an awkward toast and grimaced like he'd just shit himself.

She took Finn's hand and led him back into the house. Once across the threshold she burst out laughing. "Oh shit. That old fart will be talking about that for weeks. I think our secret's out."

"I didn't know it was a secret."

She stared at him. "No. No, it's not."

By the time they finished making love on the kitchen floor, more coals had to be piled into the grill, more lighter fluid splashed in. Another match lit.

An hour later, Jem pushed away from the table, half of her steak still on the bone. "Oh hell, that was amazing."

"Not going to finish?"

"My stomach is telling me to take this dive back into carnivorous eating one step at a time. At least I don't feel nauseated when I remember all the horrible tales of slaughterhouses that Gerald used to tell me."

"Well that's not polite dinner conversation."

"No. It wasn't. But it got the results he wanted. Me to be more like him."

Finn put his knife and fork across his plate and drummed his fingers on the table. "That's the first time I've heard resentment in your voice."

"I know more now. I see him clearer. I still loved the man. But I've taken off the rose coloured glasses." She huffed. "Hell, I've thrown them on the ground and crushed them under my feet."

"What did you first love about him?"

She stared at the crimson liquid in her wine glass. "He was brilliant. Outspoken. Beautiful and driven and…," she looked at Finn, "…odd. I loved that he was so different. The whole dance-to-the-beat-of-his-own-drum thing was endearing."

"That's what you need to remember. I'm not sure the rest matters anymore."

She ran her tongue over her teeth and squinted. "You want me to remember why I loved him? Are you weird or something?"

"Maybe. And yes, you should remember why. Keep the good in your heart, in your memories. Let the rest go or it'll eat at you. That's not good for either of us."

"Wow. You are something else, Mr. Wight."

He poured her another glass of wine. "That's Detective Wight to you." He winked, then stood and picked up their plates. "Let me clean up. Then tell me what you've learned. It might help the ca—. Help nirvana." He put the dishes on the counter then took her by the hand, her wine in his other. He guided her to the living room, set her glass down on the coffee table and pressed the power button on the remote. "Relax. I'll be quick."

The television blinked to life. Finn sauntered back into the kitchen and turned on the tap.

Who could she thank for bringing him into her life? He was perfect. No, no one is perfect. But he was perfect enough. She dropped onto the sofa and lay back on a cushion.

The couch creaked. She blinked a few times. Finn sat on the other end, her feet in his lap. The room was in darkness except for an old movie flashing television light on the walls.

He squeezed her feet. "You fell asleep."

"Sorry."

"Don't be. You must have needed it." He slid behind her and slipped his arm under her, shifting her body until she was cupped into his frame. Within seconds his breath became long and slow and quiet snores escaped his nose.

She smiled and kissed his hand that she was holding under her chin. There, not perfect. He snored. She drifted into sleep with him.

"Jem, wake up."

She slit her eyes. Still dark. The television still flickered eerie light. They were still on the couch. "What time is it?"

"I'm not sure. I guess nirvana tomorrow night?"

"Yeah. Sorry. Do you have to go?"

"No. But my arm is dead wood. Let's go upstairs."

"Okay." She swung her legs to the floor, sat up and stretched. Finn shook his arm and sat up behind her. She leaned into him and twisted around, her hand cupping his cheek. "Is that the only wood that's dead?"

He grinned. "Definitely. All other wood fully functional."

"Fantastic. I want my third helping of meat."

He pulled her hair back and chewed on her neck. "How do you want it?" he whispered in her ear.

"Raw."

not dead yet

Jem awoke to the five o'clock alarm. She stretched her arm behind her and sought Finn's warmth. All she found were cold sheets. She bolted upright.

"Finn?"

Silence.

She tossed on her robe and ran down the stairs. The aroma of fresh coffee wafted up to greet her. A piece of paper, folded in half and standing like a tent next to the full carafe of dark roast, had her name printed on it in large block letters. She unfolded it and leaned her back against the counter.

Had to run. Didn't want to wake you. Okay, I did want to, but you need to sleep sometime. 'Til tonight. XO Finn.

His wife was nuts to let him go.

She stood at the kitchen window and looked out into the yard. Two black squirrels chased each other around the trunk of the cherry tree, up onto the fence, and then flew through the air. They landed on a branch before disappearing into the leaves. Their raucous squeaks told of their delight. Or maybe they were killing each other. Adorable either way.

It was a BLT kind of day. With every mouthful of steak she'd relished the night before, her thoughts wandered to bacon. The minute it hit the fry pan, the smell overwhelmed her salivary glands.

Before the fat drained on the paper towel, she shoved a piece in her mouth.

Sorry pigs. You taste too good.

Jem held her breath and turned the van onto the street that fronted the park. The crouching form of Joe was tucked into his shrub. She exhaled and let out a nervous laugh. She unloaded the van and went straight for him.

"Joe, you scared me. Where did you go?"

He was clean, the faint smell of soap rising above the stink of his clothes. His hair shorn, his face shaven. His eyes had a flash of spark. He sat in his usual spot but his cap and jacket lay on the ground at his side. He pointed across the street to the huge homeless shelter and nodded.

"Good for you. I hope you got a hot meal or two and a good sleep." She put a hand on his shoulder. "You look wonderful."

He smiled. An actual smile, with yellowed teeth and all. He held out his hand.

"Oh, of course. Here, two of everything."

He tucked one sandwich, one juice box, and one apple under his coat. He unwrapped the other sandwich, took a big bite, and gave her a thumbs up.

She laughed, her head light and giddy. He was here, he was fine. He was better than she'd ever seen him. "I'll be right back as soon as I deliver to everyone else."

"Hey Ruby." Angus stood up and came to meet her. "He's back. I mean, we didn't think we'd ever see the guy again. Gotta say, kinda relieved, you know?"

"Yes, I do know. He seems to be coming around more and more. Have you tried talking with him?"

"Nah. Frankie welcomed him back last night. He never said

nothing. Just stared at him. But he did nod. So that's something."

"Yes, it is."

"I think he only wants you to talk to him. Maybe he's got a crush on ya, Rubes."

"I doubt that. But maybe he needed a friend. I bet if you guys took some time, he might come around."

"Maybe. Maybe. What's on the menu today?"

"BLTs, Frank's favourite. Where is he?"

"Taking a crap."

"Too much information, Angus. Too much information."

She made her rounds through the park, packed the wagon into the van, and went back to Joe. He was finishing a banana, the parchment paper folded, empty juice box sitting atop it like a paperweight.

He tapped the ground in front of him with one hand. An invitation. She sat cross-legged and smiled at him. With the filth, the facial hair, and the cap gone, scars were visible on his face. A three-inch line snaked from his right ear to the middle of his cheek. Another started above the right eyebrow and disappeared into his hairline. She reached out to touch it.

He leaned away as her finger neared.

She pulled back. "I'm sorry. But what happened to you?" She scanned his arms and hands, marred by similar marks. Why hadn't she noticed that before? Her gaze shifted to the folded pile of his brown canvas jacket.

She took his hands and ran her fingers over the scars. He didn't pull away. She turned them palm up. Pink lines bisected his forearms near the wrist. Not low enough to threaten his life, but maybe that was his plan.

"Oh, Joe. Please tell me you don't want to die. Someone has to be out there looking for you. Someone who loves you."

He shook his head and pulled his hands away then dropped his chin to his chest. "No." The word squeaked out from his underused voice box. "No one."

"Gerald didn't consider my feelings when he left, did he? Didn't ask what I wanted. Whether or not I wanted him to stay. Just up and left. Is that what you did, Joe?"

He didn't move his head, but his eyes rolled up to look at her.

"Don't make assumptions about what others want. What other people think. Because I'm telling you, you're probably wrong." Her body tensed and she ground her teeth together. "Sorry, Joe. I'm angry. At Gerald. He left. He died. And I don't know why." She licked her lips, salty from her tears. "Joe, it's not too late. You're not dead yet."

life was random

"Hello, tall, dark and meaty."

Finn's laughter on the other end of the cell phone was music in her ears. 'Sexual Healing' kind of music. 'I wanna kiss you all over' kind of music. 'I believe in miracles' kind of music.

"What time will you be here tonight? I'm thinking roast chicken and mashed potatoes with gravy."

He moaned. "That sounds amazing. But I can't come. We've got a missing child. Parent abduction. It's all hands on deck."

Her heart sank. "Of course. Will you update me? Let me know if you find — her? Him?"

"Her. And yes, I'll do that. Roast the chicken without me."

"Nah, we'll save it for tomorrow. Assuming you can come. Positive thoughts for the little girl."

He sighed. "Thanks for understanding. No wonder you're called Jem."

She groaned. "Oh, that was lame. Or sweet. Not sure which."

"Let's go with sweet. Talk soon."

She ended the call and stared at her phone. She rubbed her greasy cheek print from the screen onto her pants and tossed the phone onto the kitchen table.

The 'messages waiting' indicator flashed on her land line. She poked in her password and listened to four in a row from the office.

When will she be back? Cases piling up. Clients are pissed off they've been fobbed off on other litigators. Ugh. She leaned back in the chair and ran both hands through her hair. That part of her life seemed a million miles away. They weren't miles she wanted to traverse, not a gap she had any desire to close.

The stack of unopened mail taunted her. She sifted through each piece, tossed them onto the table unopened, like a massive deck of cards and she was dealing a game of five bill stud. Where everyone was a loser.

Near the bottom of the stack was an envelope from the insurance company. She turned it over in her hands. It couldn't be a cheque already? She ripped it open and took out a letter dated a week earlier.

She skimmed the page, key phrases popped out from the text. Suspicious circumstances of his death. In contact with police. Claim may be delayed or denied.

Well shit. She didn't kill him. How could they deny the claim?

She glanced at the clock. Another two hours before the letter carrier would shove another batch through her slot. She tossed the letter aside. Maybe work would have to come sooner than later. She had pushed the boundaries of 'as much time as you need' to her full advantage and beyond. But not today. Today would be a day to catch up on the mundane.

She gathered laundry and shoved towels into the washer, ran a vacuum around the whole house, tidying as she went. Then a quick dust and a couple more loads of dirty clothes and towels. Kitchen and bathrooms got a spit shine and de-griming. Three hours later she surveyed her home. Gerald would be proud.

She shook her head and crossed her arms. Time to stop worrying about what he would think. He'd lied to her all these years. Didn't trust her with the intimate details of his life. But he told Dean.

Everything. Damn it all to hell.

She sat in front of the music collection. Each CD came out of its rightful alphabetic place in the wire tower and landed on the hardwood. She pushed them around the floor to shuffle them, like a kid with not enough hand-eye coordination shuffled playing cards. Then she picked each one up and put them back in the tower. No order. No need for it. Life was random. CDs could be too.

The tin mail slot clinked and a new batch of bills landed in a scattered pile in her front entry. They could wait.

In the kitchen, she stripped the cupboards of all the vegan foods she'd never liked. Things she only continued to buy and choke down after Gerald disappeared because it's what he wanted from her. She flung a bag of chia seeds into the garbage. The plastic can rattled and rocked before settling back in place.

Take that, veganism.

She pulled all the tofu products from the fridge and lined them up along the counter. Silken, firm, fake cheese, fake pepperoni, fake, fake, fake. She picked up each one in turn and lobbed them into the can with the seeds. The first three shots were nothing but net. The fourth she stood right over the can and heaved with both hands. The fifth she slam-dunked.

The last bag on the counter was the dreaded mung beans. Gerald would sprout them, take up an entire shelf in the fridge with these tasteless, slimy, venus-fly-trapesque bits of grass. He'd eat them like popcorn, and the house would stink of the gas he produced. How long had she had this bag? Pigs would have to sprout wings before she'd ever sprout these damn beans again.

She snatched the bag, tossed it up and grabbed it in mid-air, spun around and winged it at the garbage can. It clipped the rim and crashed onto the floor. The cellophane burst and beans scattered across the kitchen, under the fridge and stove, and into the front entry.

Jem stared at the mess and laughed. She slid down the cupboard until her butt hit the floor. The humour left her. She was cleansing herself of all the things he loved. All the things he cared about more than he cared about her. And it hurt.

But there was no point in stopping now.

She swept up the visible beans and emptied them into the garbage. The bag was heavy with wasted food. She had no guilt over the waste, she needed it out of the house. She hauled it to the back alley and dropped it into the black bin.

Jem passed the unopened mail in the front entry and headed up the stairs. She pulled her latest memory box from the bedroom closet, a plastic container with a fastened lid that gathered the dust destined for the contents inside. She set it on her bed and popped the handles open.

The most important moments of her life rested in the half-filled box. Or at least ones she had physical mementos of. Four more boxes were stacked in the basement, labeled with the years those memories spanned. Memories she still had in her head but feared would disappear one day if she beat the family odds and lived long enough for senility to set in.

She'd already passed one test. She didn't swallow a bottle of pills when her lover died. Now she had to avoid heart disease. With her meat-loving ways back in full swing and a complete disdain for any form of exercise, that might be challenging.

Finn's fit body flashed through her mind. Maybe he would teach her. Help her. She ran a hand across her midsection. She could do better. For herself. For him.

She picked up the framed photo from the nightstand. Gerald's smiling face beamed at the camera, his hand on her shoulder. Her left hand rested on his, the engagement ring on display. What a corny pose. So predictable. So Gerald.

She wiped the dust off and placed a gentle kiss on his face, then rested the photo inside the box. She eyed the mahogany chest on the dresser. Its presence tormented her, a daily reminder of his last message to her. 'Don't want my meds. Don't want you either. Goodbye forever.' At least that was her interpretation. She dusted the top and placed the whole thing, spilled meds, abandoned ring and all, into the memory box.

She wandered about the house snatching trinkets and photos and anything Gerald-related that stood in plain sight — awards and medals and plaques for excellence in his field. She unearthed notes he'd written that she'd tucked between the pages of books to hold her place. She dusted it all and hid it away.

Finn was already up to his eyeballs in the details of Gerald's death, he didn't have to be confronted with Gerald's life. And despite what Finn said, he didn't need to be hit over the head with what Gerald meant to her. And neither did she. It was over. Time to tuck it in a corner. She could look to the past, visit the dead, if and when she needed to. Time to get on with the living.

She booted up her laptop and paid the stack of bills. Her savings were dwindling fast. If she didn't get back to work she'd have to dip into her retirement funds.

The setting sun poured in through the French doors. Angry growls came from her stomach and she glanced at the clock. Seven already. She eyed the fridge and the stove. Energy drained from her.

She poured a glass of wine into a tumbler, added a handful of ice and tossed a bag of popcorn into the microwave. She loved popcorn but hated the dirty, wet dog smell that permeated the house. But tonight, it was the perfect choice.

She took a big swig of cooled Shiraz and stared at the bag spinning in the oven. A small smile crept up on her. Gerald would have gone ballistic. Popcorn for dinner. It was one more step in releasing him. She pulled the popcorn bag open and dumped it into a bowl.

She rubbed her abdomen and her father's face appeared before her.

"I'll do better tomorrow, Dad. I promise."

She settled at the table with her laptop and Googled 'post traumatic stress disorder.' About two-hundred-ninety-three million results. She clicked through a variety of sites on the first page and scanned the information. A few case studies were interesting but focused on military personnel. Maybe Joe was military. But he was so reactive to any mention of family, his trauma had to be related to a spouse or his parents.

A click on an official-looking link brought her to a page from an American medical library.

"Post-traumatic stress disorder is a type of anxiety disorder," she read aloud. "It can happen after an individual sees or experiences a traumatic event that involves the threat of injury or death."

Sounds about right. She scrolled down the page until she found a list of symptoms. Reliving the event, having strong flashbacks and nightmares. Having strong reactions to events that remind someone of the trauma.

She'd never witnessed any of those things with Joe. Then again, she only saw him for a few minutes each day. Always in the morning. Maybe she'd make a midnight pass by the park and see what happened after dark.

The next category was avoidance. Emotional numbness or detachment. A lack of interest in normal activities and not showing moods. Not sure what was normal for Joe, but sitting in silence under a bush wasn't likely on the list. What about not speaking? Was that normal?

The last category included having an exaggerated startle response, hyper-vigilance and trouble sleeping. That was him in spades.

She scanned the rest of the webpage and hesitated at a discussion of a treatment known as desensitization. Encourage him to remember the traumatic event and express his feelings about it. If he faced the trauma, then over time, memories of it would become less frightening.

She was no head doctor, but maybe she should push him a bit harder. Try to find out what happened to him. And where the hell his family was.

She dialed Doctor Lewis' number, her foot tapping the tile while the phone rang once, twice, three times. After four, his damn voice mail picked up.

"Hey, Sid. It's Jemima. Listen, I've got an interesting question for you. Not about Gerald or Althea or anything. Don't worry, those worms are in their can for good. It's about a homeless man I've met. Do you think I could pick your brain about him? For old time's sake? Thanks, Sid. I'm at the same old number."

She pulled out a lined notepad from the top drawer of the sideboard. They'd never used it for dishes and silverware. It held nothing but paper and files and writing instruments and outdated computer parts. She scratched some notes from the site.

The ring of her cell phone cut the silence and she jumped. Sid.

"Hi, Sid."

"Hello, Jemima. What's this about a homeless man?"

"He's new to the park where I deliver sandwiches. I have no idea where he came from or why because he won't speak." She described her interactions with Joe and the progress she'd made so far. "I figure he's suffering from PTSD. Some of the symptoms fit. The only thing I can't figure out is the not speaking part."

"Mutism can happen in cases of trauma. It's called reactive mutism. But it's usually a childhood trauma. I'd say it's pretty rare in adults."

"Rare, but not unheard of?"

"Well, I've not witnessed it. But that doesn't mean it's not possible. He could have suffered a childhood trauma that was repressed and something triggered the memory. But it sounds like something happened more recently."

Jem chewed on the end of the pencil. "How recent?"

"It's hard to say without seeing him. But with PTSD, if that is what he has, probably more than thirty days ago. Though the mutism suggests sooner. Maybe it's not reactive. Maybe he just doesn't want to say anything. We know he can speak from the few words he's said to you. And the fact you got him to say those is pretty amazing if he really has suffered horrific trauma."

"So I should keep pushing?"

"I can't advise you on that, Jemima. It sounds like he needs help. Professional help."

"Right. Maybe I can find a therapist willing to come to the park." He didn't bite. "How about you, Sid? You're the best I know." The only one.

"I'm in Toronto right now. For another two weeks. Perhaps when I'm home. In the meantime, have you looked into missing persons cases?"

Now why didn't she think of that?

"Not yet. Thanks so much, Sid. I appreciate your help."

She ended the call and turned back to her computer. She Googled 'missing persons Alberta' and hit enter. She clicked on the first link the Google gods bestowed upon her. A missing persons search engine. The only search parameter she could enter was his first name.

She typed in 'Joseph' and clicked search. Eight results. That was manageable. The link for the first missing Joseph took her to a new page. An old picture of a man who was not her Joe smiled from the screen. Last seen twenty-seven years ago. Missing that long and his family was still looking for him. There was hope for Joe yet.

She visited the site of each missing Joseph, scanned the date they went missing, the description, the photos. He wasn't among them. Or at least she didn't think so. He was so thin. None of these men were emaciated. What did Joe look like with some meat on his bones? What was normal for him?

A numbing thought hit her. Maybe he wasn't from Alberta. He could be from anywhere, even the States. She rubbed her forehead, covered her mouth with her hand, and stared at the screen. She needed help.

She shut down her laptop, refilled her tumbler with wine and ice, and took the bowl of popcorn into the living room. Her body sank into the sofa and she grabbed the remote.

Page after page of choices flashed on the screen, three hundred channels of crap. The digital video recorder she'd bought two years after Gerald's disappearance had done little to fill the void in her life, but it did kill some time. She chose *Dirty Dancing* for the umpteenth time. She could quote lines in her sleep. Familiar faces and familiar feelings let her escape from her life for a few moments. And the wine made her eyelids heavy.

A sharp rap at the window next to her head jolted her awake. Finn's face was pressed up against the glass.

"I knocked but you didn't answer," he called through the closed window. "Saw the TV flickering."

"Holy shit you scared me to death." She let him in the front door. "I think it's time I gave you a key. What time is it?"

"Four-thirty. Sorry, but we found her."

Jem cocked her head to one side. "You mean the missing little girl? That's wonderful."

"Hell yeah it is. Mother was trying to take her into Montana. Border agents got her and the Mounties brought her back here. The girl is with her father."

"Why?"

"Why what?"

"Why isn't the mother allowed to have her daughter?"

"Because she's a drug addict and hooker. She leaves her five-year-old alone all night while she's out turning tricks and getting high."

"Oh. Good reason."

"I wanted to let you know. And I can't sleep. Never can after something like this. It's like a great bennie high."

She raised one eyebrow. "And you would know this how?"

"Youthful indiscretions." He gathered her in his arms and kissed her. "Do I smell popcorn?"

"That was dinner."

"Yikes. I'll be here tomorrow, promise. In the meantime," he pulled away from her. "I'll let you go back to sleep."

She grabbed the lapel of his jacket and pulled him back. She eyed the jacket and rubbed the fabric between her thumb and fingers. "Is that silk?"

"Yeah."

"A cop in a silk suit?"

"Only the jacket. See, jeans."

She took a step back. "Wow. Casual and buttoned down all at the same time." She took hold of his lapel again. "But I'm supposed to get up in half an hour, so no point in sleeping now." She slid the jacket off his shoulders and tossed it over the armchair, pointed at him, then beckoned him with a come-hither gesture. She flashed her eyebrows up and down and ran up the stairs, Finn on her heels.

a dangerous game

Jem hauled the sandwich box out into a gleaming June morning and loaded it into her van. She tiptoed upstairs and peeked in the bedroom door. Finn lay naked and sound asleep in her bed, covers thrown off, the rising sun illuminating his muscular frame.

Less than two hours ago, the moment he climaxed, he rolled off her and passed out, the post-arrest high satisfied by one great romp. When she came back in the room after her shower, he hadn't moved a muscle. She crept around the room, pulling drawers open an inch at a time so as not to disturb him. She could have slammed doors and screamed bloody murder, she doubted he would notice. He was dead to the world after more than twenty-four hours without a break.

And here he was, still in the same spot, an hour after her time in the kitchen making tuna sandwiches. One arm above his head, the other thrown out to the side, one leg straight, the other slightly bent and flopped to one side. The view was breathtaking.

He was like no man she'd ever been with. It was more than the whole Greek God good looks thing. It was everything about him. He was so thoughtful. So kind. So sweet. So, so... So horny.

She licked her lips and approached the side of the bed. His signature little snores made her want him again. She ran one finger from his ankle to his groin and up to his chest.

His eyes popped open and he became erect in an instant. He

grabbed her and rolled her onto the bed, pinned her shoulders and sat on her thighs. "That's a dangerous game to play with me." He bent and kissed her.

She laughed with his tongue in her mouth and then returned the kiss with vigor. Adrenaline-soaked arousal sliced through her body. She groaned and turned her head to the side. "I can't believe I'm saying this, but I don't want to have sex right now."

He released her shoulders and sat back. "Oh. Sorry." He ran his finger between her breasts, over her clothes, and scratched between her legs over her denim capris. "I got a different impression." His smile was disarming as hell.

"Let me put it this way. I do want to, but I can't. The sandwiches are in the van. Tuna. Mayonnaise. Can't leave them for long or I'll poison everybody."

"Now that I understand." He kissed her forehead. "If you wait five minutes I can shower and come with you." He climbed off of her and headed for the bathroom.

"You don't have to go to work?"

"Nope. Day off."

"Maybe you should sleep."

"I can do that later. Unless you don't want me to come. I mean, this is your thing, I get that. I don't want to intrude." He stood sideways in the bathroom doorway, one hand on the jamb, eyebrows raised.

She stared at him for a few seconds. "I would love for you to come."

He beamed and turned away. The shower started to run, the door still wide open.

She skipped down the stairs and poured them each a cup of coffee.

He fastened his watch on the way down the stairs. A dark grey t-shirt taut against his chest hung loose around his hips. He wasn't even tucked in today. He slid bare feet into flip-flops.

Casual Finn was even hotter than suit-and-tie Finn. Giving him a drawer to keep a few changes of clothes was the best idea she'd ever had.

She handed him a travel mug and a granola bar and kissed his cheek. They climbed into the van and she pulled away from the curb.

"Maybe don't tell anyone you're a cop. It might scare some of them off."

"Done."

"Gotta say, even dressed like that, you have cop tattooed on your forehead."

He snickered. "So I've been told. How about I hang back at the van. Let you go ahead with the deliveries. If you want me to come closer, give me a signal."

"I like that idea. There's one fellow in particular I'm worried about. He's pretty new, and he doesn't speak. I'm making progress with him, got him to tell me his name. And he did answer a question yesterday. Only a couple of words mind you, but still, with a voice. He hasn't talked to any of the others in the park."

"Got it. Don't mess with the residents."

"Joe is different than the others. I think his family might be looking for him but I have no way of finding out."

Finn turned to her. "Jem, you've got a detective sitting right beside you. Finding shit out is what I do."

She glanced at him. "I didn't know how to ask. It's not a case. Unless there's a missing persons report or something. I looked online but couldn't see anyone that resembled Joe. I don't even know where he came from."

"We have better resources than the internet. Let me take a look at him — from a distance."

"Thank you." She put her hand on his knee. "I bet Frank and Angus would love you. You'll get a huge kick out of them."

"Were they there a couple of years ago? When you saw Gerald?"

"Yes. Angus has been hanging his hat in the park for four years. Frank even longer. Why?"

"I think I might have interviewed them. Part of the investigation. Them and a few others."

"I forgot about that. So they know you're a cop already."

"Only if they remember me. I won't say anything."

Jem pulled into her usual spot and parked. Finn lifted the wagon from the van, filled it with boxes of food and drink, then hoisted the entire thing over the curb and put the handle in her hand.

She watched him and grinned. "I might get used to you doing all the heavy lifting. Maybe you should come with me more often."

"I could arrange that." He bent and kissed her cheek.

She started on the far side of the park. "Hi Joe. Beautiful morning, isn't it?" She knelt in front of him. "Tuna today."

Joe stared past her. She turned around and glanced at Finn.

"It's okay. That's my boyfriend." That was the first time she'd said that out loud. Or even thought about it. Her boyfriend. How odd.

Joe's posture slackened and he looked at his sandwich. He glanced up at her as he unwrapped the parchment and took a bite. She was rewarded with his now-daily thumbs up.

Question after question stalled on her lips. Today was not the day to push. With Finn here making him nervous, too much prodding might send him back where he came from. She stood there for a couple of minutes to be sure he ate his food and tucked his seconds away for later before making her way around the park.

Frank and Angus waited for her to get to the other side. They sat with straight backs, their gazes shifting from her to Finn.

"Good morning, gentlemen."

"Ruby. Why'd you bring that cop with you?"

"You remember him?"

"Hell yeah, hard to forget. Bit rough around the edges."

She grinned. "Not when you get to know him. He's been investigating Gerald's disappearance all these years. He's cool."

"Gee, Jem." Frank looked at his feet. "We're starting to think you don't love us anymore."

"How so?"

"First Chief comes along and steals all your attention. Then you bring this big dude around. Not looking so cop-like today, is he?" The light glinted off Frank's good eye, a sly smile crept onto his face.

She put her arm around his shoulder and gave him half a hug. "Ah, Frank. No one will ever replace the two of you in my heart."

"Cop-man replaced Gerald though, didn't he?" Frank elbowed her in the ribs.

"We have started... seeing each other. But no one will ever replace Gerald. I've just added Finn to the fold, you know?"

Angus eyed Finn over her shoulder. She turned and followed his glare. Finn leaned against the passenger side of the van, looking at his phone. Who the hell was he texting? He was supposed to be checking out Joe, helping her figure out who he was.

She looked to Joe. He hadn't moved a muscle. He watched Finn too, but not with curiosity like Angus. More like with dread. Had Finn spooked Joe? Maybe she shouldn't have brought him with her.

"Is he good to you, Ruby?"

"Yes he is. And thank you for worrying about me."

"You're my girl, Ruby. Always will be."

"I love you too, Angus."

She glanced back at Finn, he was still looking at his phone.

Damn it, who was so interesting that he didn't care about Joe? Wait, was she jealous? Of a text? It was probably work-related. Something about a case. Get a grip, Jem.

He put the phone to his ear.

What the hell? Couldn't they leave him alone on his day off?

For the first time since they'd started, what, dating? No. Having a relationship? How could she define what they had? Friends with benefits? Really, really amazing benefits. Whatever it was called, this is the first time she was annoyed with him. She balled her hands into fists and bounced them off her thighs. Maybe he hadn't understood how important finding Joe's family was to her.

She shook her head and admonished herself under her breath. That's how his wife reacted. Jealous of his work, of his cases. Jem couldn't let that happen, couldn't be like the ex. This is who he was, accept it or end it.

Finn held his phone up at arm's length and squinted like he was farsighted. She'd never noticed that before. He didn't wear glasses. Never took contacts out at night. She shook her head. He looked adorable and sexy and strong and vulnerable.

No way was she going to end it.

"Well guys, I'm out of here for today. Any requests for tomorrow?"

"Bacon."

"Oh Frank, we've got to find you a new favourite."

She met Finn on the sidewalk.

"How's Joe?" He picked up the wagon and loaded it into the van.

"Seems fine. He's a bit freaked out by you. I didn't push him for information. One thing at a time, right?"

They got into the van and she pulled away from the curb.

"I got a couple of pictures of him. Not sure how good they'll turn out on this phone, and from that distance. Tried to be all casual like I was texting or something. Didn't work. Had to hold it out like an old fart reading the Sunday paper."

Well damn. She was an idiot. All annoyance melted from her.

"I called in a favour. Gave a colleague a starter description and sent the photos. If you can get more info, that'd be great. Maybe you could get a shot closer up?"

"Maybe. He'd hate that. I don't think he wants to be found. But he did go to the shelter, showered and shaved. So maybe he's coming around."

Finn reached up and rested his forearm on the back of her headrest. "Do you realize we've never been out on a date?"

Interesting change of topic. "What, barbecue and endless sex doesn't count?"

He snickered and ran his fingers down the back of her neck. She shivered.

"I think you should know I've never slept with a woman on the first date before."

"You married your high school sweetheart. How many dates have you had since she left?"

"Counting tonight?"

Her heart leapt. "Tonight?"

"Yeah. We're going out. Anywhere you want. And this will bring my post-divorce tally to one."

"You haven't had one date since she left?"

"I haven't had a date, not a first one anyway, since grade ten."

She stole a glance at him. She was only his second relationship? He wasn't her second. She'd been, let's just say, active before she met Gerald. But Finn didn't need to know that.

"I don't know what to say."

"I guess I'm particular about who I ask out. What do you want to do?"

She drummed her fingertips on the steering wheel. "Dinner. And a movie." She nodded. "Yeah, that's what I want. But we need to sit in the back corner."

"Why?"

"Since you don't sleep with women on the first date, then I'm not gettin' any tonight. So the least you can do is grope me in the theatre."

He laughed and squeezed her neck. "I can do that. And maybe I can break the first date rule too."

"Excellent."

They pulled up in front of her house. Finn grabbed the empty boxes from the back and met her on the doorstep.

Jem pushed open the front door. More mail littered the entry. She stooped to collect it, and piled it on top of the other envelopes waiting for her attention. "Coffee?"

"Sure." Finn fingered the stack of mail. "Jem, how are you doing?"

"I'm fine. Why?" She slid a filter into the coffee pot. His arm came over her shoulder and the stack of mail landed on the countertop in front of her.

"You seem to be avoiding things. We haven't talked about nirvana in days. You were going to tell me what you learned about Gerald, but every time I bring it up, you find a way to put it off." He rubbed her shoulders and bent his head towards hers. "I'm worried about you," he whispered in her ear. He kissed her cheek and spun her around.

She buried her face in his chest and hugged him. "I know. I wish it would be done. Find his killer, answer all the questions, move on and forget. The bad stuff I mean."

"We'll get there. Maybe not all the questions can be answered, they usually aren't. It's not like on television where every loose end is conveniently tied in one moment of clarity from one clue. Doesn't work that way." He pulled back and put his hands on either side of her face, then landed a sweet kiss on her nose. "Gerald was a pretty complex guy. The case is complicated by his disease. I think the murder might be the easiest part to close. And at this point, it's the only thing being investigated. His disappearance was solved with the discovery of his body. But that doesn't help you, doesn't explain why he left." He cupped her chin in one hand and kissed her lips. "How can I help you?"

She swallowed and pushed down tears. "You help me every day. By being here, being with me. You're a miracle. And I don't believe in miracles, so that's big mister." She poked his chest, and then buried her face in it again. "Speaking of putting it off." She tilted her head back, rested her chin on his chest, and leered up at him. "You wanna fuck?"

"Yes. Always. But not now." He took her hand and grabbed the pile of mail. "You catch up on this, I'll make the coffee. We'll talk about what you learned at the funeral. Then it's out of the way."

"All right. You're right. Get it done and over with."

"And then we'll fuck."

She patted his cheek. "That's my boy."

She sat at the table and picked up the mail. One pile for bills. One pile for junk. One pile for other. Near the bottom, another insurance company envelope caught her attention. More delays? More questions? She tapped the short edge on the table and ripped open the other end. Two pieces of paper slid out.

"Oh my God." She put a hand to her mouth.

Finn turned and put a cup of coffee on the table next to her. "What is it?"

She turned the sheet around and held it by the edges between her thumbs and index fingers.

Finn's eyes widened. "Holy cow."

She turned it back and stared at it. Two-and-a-half-million dollars. All on one little piece of paper. "Wow. I didn't really believe I'd get this."

Finn picked up the letter and unfolded it. "You've been cleared of all suspicion." He put his cup down next to hers and folded the sheet again, then stuffed it into the envelope. "Of course you have. I signed the declaration."

"You did? When?"

"Couple of weeks ago."

She stared at the cheque. Ran her fingers over the ink.

He pulled a chair out and sat across from her. "What are you going to do? Shopping spree? Big trip around the world?"

"No, nothing so frivolous. Pay off the mortgage. And I have an idea but I have to think it through." She had to call the office. And go to the bank.

Finn leaned back in his chair. His eyes drooped and his body slouched. Very un-Finn like.

"You look exhausted. Go up and get some sleep before dinner."

He shook his head. "Nirvana."

Right. Deal with it now, Jemima. He won't sleep until you do. She nodded and steeled herself.

"Gerald's father did not have a heart attack."

"No?" Finn sat up, his eyes bright and aware, like he had a switch he could flick on any time he needed to.

She held her mug with both hands and looked into the steaming liquid. "He committed suicide. Hung himself in the basement."

"Oh, shit. Do they know why?"

"He didn't leave a note. But he'd been acting odd for years. Paranoid. Seeing things that weren't there. Listening to inanimate

145

objects. Sound familiar?"

"So he was schizophrenic too."

"No one will say that. He was never diagnosed. It was twenty-four years ago. Maybe the medical community is better about that kind of thing now. Or maybe Althea shoved her head in the sand back then too. But diagnosed or not, it all sounds like Gerald." She picked at a non-existent spot on her arm. "Gerald knew. He found him. Hanging from a beam. When he was only thirteen."

Finn pushed back into the chair. "Oh hell. That's enough all on its own to mess with a kid's brain." He leaned forward again, forearms on the table and shook his head. "Poor guy. Can you imagine how he felt when he started acting the same way as his father?"

"Finn, Gerald was thirty-three when he disappeared. His dad was thirty-four when he died." Tears streamed down her face. "Did he leave to protect me? Was he going to kill himself?"

"But he didn't. Four years later and he hadn't done that. Even sought help for part of that time."

"But he didn't come back." She ran a hand through her hair and emptied her lungs. "I don't understand."

"You may never understand. The only one who did was Gerald. And maybe he didn't either. Maybe the others guided him and his choices. Jem, he was gone long before he left."

She burst into tears. Finn gathered her in his arms and rocked her until she stopped. She pulled away. "I'm okay. I am." She wiped her cheeks. "But thanks. For being right where I need you."

They shared a gentle kiss.

"Now you go sleep. Please? I've got some errands to run and I'll meet you back here for our first real date."

"Okay, I won't argue. I'm beat."

decadent choices

Jem dressed up, braved the peep-toed stilettos, and opted for fitted linen pants and a plunging neckline. She painted her face and curled the ends of her hair into a flip. When she came out of the bathroom Finn *rawred* at her. She wanted to drop their clothes right there and fuck all night.

He'd released something in her that had been dormant for so long. A zest for everyday life. A sexual appetite that had been gathering dust for four years and had barely been sated the two before that. She couldn't get enough.

Her arm through his, they wended their way between the tables at Rush, his favourite restaurant, and made their way towards Finn's requested booth in a far corner. He guided her ahead of him, his hand on the small of her back.

Women who caught sight of him did a double take, admired her beautiful man in black denim, pink shirt and ivory silk sports coat. Then they glanced at her with disdain. Or perhaps jealousy. Hell, even she was turning heads. More than one man gave her the up-down and a leering half-grin.

Through three courses and a bottle of wine, they sat so close their thighs were in constant contact. He fed her bits of his roasted rack of lamb and spring vegetables and she countered with an offering of maple ridge duck and butter poached asparagus. She could eat as much as she wanted, he never suggested she try the diet plate, never raised an eyebrow at her decadent choices.

They shared *les pots de chocolats* for dessert. When some of the sweet, espresso-flavoured chocolate dripped onto her chin, he licked it off and kissed her, sucked her lips and lingered, the taste of chocolate and red wine on his tongue more intoxicating than the alcohol.

The waiter slid the bill onto the table. Jem snatched it and held it away from Finn. "It's on me. Now that I'm rich and all." She scanned the bill and raised one eyebrow. "Holy shit. Good thing I'm rich. How often do you eat here?"

He put his arm around her shoulder and grabbed the bill from her hand. "Not often enough. And no way are you paying. I don't care how rich you are, the man always pays."

"How very old-fashioned of you." Her feminist side should be offended, but the princess in her enjoyed being taken care of — even if his cop salary would limit how often they dined in fancy places like Rush.

At the theatre, they chose an old movie that neither cared to see. The trailers for upcoming films had already started when they climbed the steps to the last row. They sat in the back corner out of the beam of flickering light from the projection room. Only three other people sat in the dark with them, one couple with their heads leaned together, and a loner in the front row.

Jem watched the screen, her hand held in Finn's firm grip. The stench of theatre popcorn and fake butter permeated the room. The worn tapestry of the armrest scratched against her bare elbow. Heat from his body saturated the soft silk of his suit jacket where their arms touched and sent goose bumps up her arm.

The movie started with a huge explosion, the screen flashed bright and they were bombarded by surround sound.

Finn put his hand under her chin and turned her to face him. He kissed her with an open mouth, his tongue everywhere like he was a horny teenager. He reached into her low-cut top, cupped one breast inside her bra and massaged her nipple between his thumb and finger. He dropped his head to her chest and kissed her cleavage, then pulled her breast out of her top and sucked her hardened nipple.

She gasped, her heart raced, legs jelly. She glanced at the others in the theatre. No one was paying any attention.

He looked her in the eye and winked. "Too bad you didn't wear a skirt," he whispered.

"I'll remember that for next time."

She pulled his belt open, unbuttoned his jeans and inched the zipper down. She reached inside and stroked him while they kissed.

"Slow down," he whispered. "I'm going to make a mess all over my pants."

"I can fix that." She bent forward and took him into her mouth. The armrest between them dug into her ribs as her head bobbed up and down on his erection. He moaned, his hand on the back of her head. She giggled with her mouth full of him. She felt like her old twenty-something self again.

By the time the movie was more than half over they'd been hushed three times by the couple, and the loner kept peering back at them to see what they were up to. After Finn got her to orgasm with his hand over her pants, he zipped himself up and tucked in his shirt. "Let's get out of here."

They skipped down the stairs hand-in-hand and emerged into the bright light of the lobby. Her face was hot and she could imagine how she looked — hair mussed, makeup smudged, clothing askew.

Best first date ever.

Finn pulled up in front of the house and opened the car door for her. They walked up the sidewalk with their arms around each other.

They fell into the front door, pawing each other's clothes off. Jem backed up the steps, kissing him and undoing his pants. He followed, unclasped her bra and stripped off her slacks. Halfway up the stairs he placed one arm under her lower back and the other under her neck and laid her down. She wrapped her legs around him and they had sex right there. She held the railing spindles on either side of the stairs, the carpet runner dug into her shoulder blades and lower back.

That would hurt tomorrow. But tonight it didn't matter. It was another hot installment in their great sexual adventure.

She was on the verge of full release when he pulled out and rested his forehead on her chest.

"Oh, no. Don't stop now." She pulled him forward but he resisted.

"Not stopping. Just pausing." He stood and pulled her to her feet, took her hand and ran up the stairs to her bedroom. He jumped on the bed and dragged her behind him. He reached over and dug his hand in the top drawer of her night table and pulled out a condom. "That was a little too close for comfort."

She laughed.

"Maybe I should carry one of these in every pocket."

After a long session of sweaty sex, they lay in darkness, her head in that wonderful nook at the intersection of his shoulder and collarbone. Her spot.

"Finn?"

"Yeah, baby?"

Baby? He'd never called her that before. It was good.

"I quit today."

"Smoking?"

She hadn't lit a cigarette in days. Not since the night before Gerald's funeral. "No. Well, yeah, I guess I did that too. But that's not it." She pushed herself up on one elbow and drew random patterns on his chest with one finger. "I quit my job."

"What?" He put his hand over hers. "Why?"

"I'm going to keep practicing, but on my own. I budgeted it out. After I pay off the mortgage I can run a small practice from home. All pro-bono work. You know, for people who can't afford lawyers."

He smiled at her, his face warm and soft. "Now why doesn't that surprise me?"

"I could defend people who are actually innocent. I'd get to hand-pick the cases. And I have enough to keep up the sandwich deliveries too."

"Well, I'm glad you aren't giving that up." He kissed the top of her head then dropped his head onto the pillow, his lips drawn in a thin line.

"You look skeptical. Don't you trust me?"

"Not skeptical. But a bit worried. I know that insurance money sounds like a lot, but isn't it expensive to run a law practice? Aren't there court costs and such to pay?"

"Yes. I have to be careful. As time goes on, I may need to take paying clients." She squeezed his hand. "But it would be my choice of cases. My hours. I could turn the second bedroom into an office. And the best part? No damn partners."

He nodded. "Sounds like you've got a good plan."

She laid her head on his chest. "It sounds perfect to me."

someone who needs him

Jem pulled the empty wagon behind her and left the park. Joe still wasn't talking, but without Finn around, he was more relaxed. Tomorrow she'd start asking harder questions. Try to trigger something, a memory, an admission. Anything.

She slid the van into drive as her phone's text alert chimed. Finn's name flashed on the screen and she grinned. Would she ever stop feeling like a school girl with her first crush? Ever get used to the fact that he wanted to be with her, that he liked her? Maybe even loved her. She pushed the gearshift back into park and opened the message.

'News about Joseph. You at the park?'

'Yes, just leaving.'

'Coming home?'

'Be there in less than fifteen minutes.'

'I'll put on a pot of coffee.'

She couldn't stop grinning the entire trip. He didn't call it her home. Not her house. Just home.

His car was parked out front when she arrived, far enough down the block that he left her usual spot free.

He met her on the sidewalk, opened the side door of the van and retrieved the wagon. "I'm not sure, but I think we might have found Joe."

"We?"

"Yeah, me and that colleague I told you about. She's waiting inside."

"She?"

He turned and looked at her. "Yes. Detective Anders. Why?"

"No reason. I guess I imagined you working with a bunch of rough-around-the-edges men. Dumb, huh?"

"Yeah, a little." He put his arm around her shoulder and drew her in for a long kiss.

In the kitchen, a striking woman sat at the table, a mug of steaming coffee at her elbow. She stood when Jem entered, towering over her a good four inches.

The woman held out her hand. "So you're the famous Jemima? Finn's talked of nothing else for months. You know, your case and your fiancé's disappearance."

Jem shook her hand. Tall, blonde and built. Fitted suit, sharp crease pressed into each pant leg. And those legs went for miles. Like a female Finn. What factory did this city custom-order its perfect detectives from?

"Nice to meet you. You've been looking for information on Joseph, Detective Anders?"

"Beryl, please."

Finn handed Jem a coffee and pulled out a chair for her. She glanced down at her khaki skirt, black tank top and hoodie. How the hell could she compete with the likes of Beryl? How was he not ripping her clothes off every night instead of Jem's? It was better when she didn't know other people in his life. Better to let her imagination fill his world with gruff men with big bellies and no women at all. It was only a matter of time before his attentions turned to someone prettier, thinner, smarter.

"Jem." Finn put his hand on her arm. "You okay?"

"Huh?" She looked up to find him watching her, one eyebrow arched high. "Sorry, I'm a little tired." She turned to Beryl. "What about Joe?"

Beryl pulled some papers from a manila file. "We haven't found out who he is, don't have enough to go on yet. But we've got some photos for you to look at."

Jem took the four pictures and spread them out. She eliminated two of them based on the eyes alone. She picked a third and studied the face. A handsome man, maybe mid-thirties with short, sandy hair and straight, white teeth smiled back at her. His eyes looked grey. She flipped the paper over. A description on the back claimed his eyes were blue, his hair blonde, and his height six foot four. She tossed that one aside.

"Not him either?" Finn sipped his coffee.

"Too tall. I've never seen him stand up, but when I sit in front of him I almost look him in the eye. Not like you, I have to tip my head back to look at you."

Beryl huffed air from her nose. Jem looked from her to Finn. He was blushing.

She picked up the last picture, and read the back first. Five foot ten, one hundred eighty pounds. Eyes light blue, hair dark blonde, thirty one years old. Missing since last November. From Regina.

She turned it back over and looked into Joe's face. Her heart missed a beat and she sat straight in her chair. No scars, more meat on his bones, but no mistaking it. That was him. The crook on the bridge of his nose, the slight gap between his front teeth, the smattering of freckles on his cheeks.

"That's him. That's Joseph."

Finn took the photo. "Are you sure?"

"Almost definitely. I mean he's thin as a rail now, and scarred. I might have missed it if he hadn't shaved and cut his hair. But I think so."

She snatched the photo back and turned it over again. "Joseph Carlisle." She looked at Finn and broke into a wide smile, then jumped up and hugged him. "Thank you. For giving him a name."

"Thank Beryl. I just showed her the lousy cell phone pictures."

She hugged Beryl. "Thank you too. I mean it. I knew he had family somewhere. Someone who needs him." Tears filled her eyes. "What's next?"

Beryl took Joe's picture and looked at the back. "I'll get in touch with the Regina police, see what they can tell me. I'll keep you posted."

"Anders, can I catch up with you in the car?"

Beryl grinned. "You bet, Wight. Toss me the keys."

Finn fished keys from his jacket pocket and lobbed them in the air. Beryl caught them overhand and turned to leave. She looked over her shoulder. "Don't be too long." She winked.

When the door closed, Jem turned to him. "What the hell was that about?"

He pulled her to him and kissed her. Every jealous bone in her body broke on impact. A full minute went by before he released her and brushed hair from her eyes. "When I pulled out a key and let myself into your house, I kind of had to explain."

She smoothed his lapels. "I see. So I was a secret?"

"No, not a secret. But other than the case, not a topic of conversation. I don't kiss and tell."

"She's beautiful."

"Anders? Yeah, I guess she looks that way."

"Looks that way?"

"Like apples in a grocery store. All shiny and perfect from far away, but up close you see it's wax hiding the bruises and wormholes."

"Wow. Quite the creepy analogy. Did you two ever date?"

He laughed. "No, definitely not. I've never looked at her that way."

"Why not?"

"She's a cop, not a dating prospect. Besides, when we first met I was married. Then I was going through a divorce. And before that was ever finalized I was kind of into you. Even though I couldn't tell you that. And you may have never reciprocated. But you did." Another gentle kiss to her lips. "And it was worth the wait."

She rested her forehead on his chest. Warmth spread through her body. "Finn?"

"Uh-huh."

She reached around and squeezed both his ass cheeks. "Define 'too long.'"

He groaned. "Don't tease me. I've got to get through the rest of this day without a hard-on."

"Too late."

green Rider pride

The next morning, Jem made her rounds through the park in the same pattern as was her habit. She resisted the urge to run up to Joe and throw her arms around him. She only knew his name and where he came from. It might be a while before the authorities in Regina gave them more.

She handed out sandwiches and avoided small-talk, glancing Joe's way every few feet. He watched her with intent. What if he figured out that she knew who he was? What if he bolted before she even got to him?

Jem tried to focus on the last few residents and had animated conversations with them about the weather, the Calgary Flames chances for a Stanley Cup bid, Flossie's new hat. Anything to appear casual and normal, even though Jem's insides were quaking with anticipation.

When she got to Joe, she sat in front of him. He met her with a big smile, that gap between his front teeth reassuring her that she'd identified the right photo.

"Morning, Joe. It's a beautiful day, isn't it?"

He nodded. She handed him his food and he unwrapped his breakfast.

"Did I tell you before that I'm a lawyer?"

He stopped mid-bite and froze in place. A second later he bit through the bread and shook his head, his eyes locked on her.

"Criminal defense. Except most of my clients are guilty. They say they're not, but they are. My win-lose record is pitiful. I'm supposed to defend them to the bitter end on the assumption that if they say they are innocent, I believe them. But I've got to admit, I usually don't."

She pulled a few blades of grass.

"You ever get arrested, Joe?"

He swallowed and sucked on his juice box, then shook his head once.

"That's good. I bet you've never done anything illegal."

He shrugged.

"I'm going to open my own law practice. Right out of my house. If you ever need a lawyer, you remember me, okay?"

He nodded.

"Have you ever been to Regina, Joe?"

He stopped moving and stared at her, that feral glint that she hadn't seen in a while returned. He nodded with one jerk of his head.

"I've only been once. Nice place I guess. Kind of small when you're used to Calgary." She leaned forward, arms on her thighs. "And their football team sucks." She laughed.

His posture relaxed and he smiled, then shook his head. "Go Riders."

His voice cracked but it came through loud and clear.

"Oh, you're a fan? A little green, Rider pride flowing through those veins?" She tapped him on the upper arm with a closed fist.

He shrugged.

"Hey, don't tell the others, but I brought you a treat." She pulled a Mars bar from her pocket. "You're not allergic to nuts or anything, are you?"

His eyes lit up. He shook his head and held out his hand.

"I'll bring you another tomorrow. Do you like that kind? Do you have a favourite?"

"Oh! Henry?"

"Oh! Henry it is."

Jem's phone vibrated in her pocket. She held up one finger to Joe and eyed the screen, her brows furrowed.

"Dean? What's up?"

Hesitation on the other end. "I need to speak with you. Can I come over?"

"Of course. I'll be home in half an hour." She listened to him breathe. "Is Anna okay? You sound terrible."

"Yes, she's fine. It's nothing like that." Silence.

"Dean, are you still there?"

He let out a heavy sigh. "It's about Gerald's will."

before I lose everything

"Damn it!" Jem sucked on her thumb where she'd hit it with a hammer.

Wooden parts, screws and nails, and sticks of balsa wood doweling littered the floor of the spare bedroom. It never failed. She'd always put one piece in wrong, then have to rip it all apart and start over. Next time, skip Ikea and get to Sears. Somewhere that the furniture comes all put together.

Where the hell was Dean? She checked her phone. No messages from him or Finn. It had been days since she'd identified Joe's picture. What was taking Beryl so long to get some answers?

The tinny chime of her old doorbell echoed in the hall. She raced down the stairs, and swung the door open. Dean stood on her doorstep, his suit jacket un-buttoned, tie loosened, hair mussed up. "Dean, you look awful." Very un-Dean-like.

He hesitated and then stepped into the entry. "Can we sit?"

"Of course. You want a beer?"

"Oh yeah, I really do."

She pulled open the fridge, pushed aside a box of Oh! Henry's and grabbed two green bottles. "Living room or kitchen?"

"Living room."

She handed him a beer and led the way, sinking into the sofa. Dean sat on the chair to her left. She pulled her feet up onto the cushion. "So, what's this about Gerald's will? I thought he didn't have one. I've already been to the bank, made the necessary changes on the mortgage and the title."

"That's fine. It's your house." He sat back and drained half the bottle in one long swig.

Her eyes narrowed. "Dean, what the hell? Tell me."

"The department had me clean out his desk three years ago so they could use it. I shoved all of his papers in a box. I figured it was a bunch of research notes, but couldn't bring myself to look at it. Forgot all about it. Until today." He ran his hand over his hair. "I found a will. Not notarized or anything. Just handwritten." He fumbled inside his jacket and pulled an envelope from the pocket. He held it out to her.

Jem raised one hand, her palm to Dean. "No. I don't want to see it. What does it say?"

"That you should have everything. He figured his mother would be dead already. If she outlived him, she could have some of his awards and commendations. Whichever ones you wanted to give her."

"I see." She looked at the shelves where those things used to gather dust.

"It had funeral instructions. I'm so sorry, Jem. I should have given you the box. Should have opened it the minute I knew he was gone. You know, for good."

Jem crossed her arms and gave herself a short hug. "I understand. I'm struggling to face it too. I've started cleaning out his things, giving away, putting away. But it's like I'm erasing him. Wiping out his existence. I can't live with the constant reminders, but I don't want him to disappear."

He nodded. "That's it exactly."

"All I've done is some of his clothes and the visible stuff.

Haven't even touched the basement."

"Do you want to know what he wanted?"

"The funeral? I know what he wanted. It wasn't what he got, but it's fine. Even if it were in his handwriting, Althea would have ignored it. Probably would have thought I put him up to it, or forged his will or something."

He heaved a sigh and slid another envelope from inside his jacket. "There's more." He tapped it on his knee. "There was this. It wasn't in an envelope, just sandwiched between some research notes." He rubbed the back of his neck. "I read it. I'm sorry."

She took the envelope and pulled out two pieces of lined paper. Gerald's tight slanted cursive jumped from both sides of the pages, his dotless Js and Is. Slowed the flow he said, stopping to stab the page above those little letters. He only crossed his Ts so they didn't look like Ls. She shut her eyes for a second, the sight of his handwriting making his presence palpable. A lump formed in her throat and a spasm gripped her stomach. She wiped tears from her cheeks. Then she swallowed and opened her eyes.

My Darling Jemima,

Do you remember the day we met? I loved you from that moment. The look on your face when we collided outside the lecture hall. You were pissed, apologetic, flustered. I didn't know then that you stormed into everything you did. That you were a force to be reckoned with. That was my favourite thing about you. Your strength. Your drive. Your ethics. I bet I never told you that.

Sometimes I don't remember. Some days the past melts away and all I can see is a bleak future. Today it is all here, all in my head. So I have to tell you all of this before it is gone again.

My father committed suicide. I'm sorry I lied to you about that. Other than family, only Dean knows. He was my best friend then as he is now, and the only person I felt could talk to. Until you came into my life.

But I didn't want you to worry. You see, Dad was sick. Like me. I mean, exactly like me. Last year when I went on meds for the first time, I could see clearly what was happening. See that I was acting the same way, doing the same things. I didn't understand it when I was a kid. I could see he was odd, but found myself scared of him often. He was erratic. He was normally calm and loving, but then he started having outbursts. He started yelling for no reason. He even hit me a few times. Called me by names I didn't understand. I get it now. He wasn't seeing me. He was seeing something else. Someone else. Someone who scared him.

I do that now. I look at you and I see someone I don't know. Someone who scares me. Not always. Not every day. But more and more often. I don't want to harm you, Jem. I couldn't live with myself. Assuming I even knew what the hell I had done.

I only realize these things when I'm on meds. Reality kicks in, even if it is wrapped in fuzziness. But I can't live on those pills. They mess with me too, just in a different way. I can't face this life without my brain intact. Without my research. Schizophrenia is robbing me of it, fast. Meds rob me of it too, only slower. Either way, it's disappearing. It defined me, my research. My intelligence. My academia. Or maybe I let it define me. Maybe I should have looked for a better definition.

Not long before we met I discovered that my grandmother was ill too. She was institutionalized in her forties. Dad was in his late teens then, and engaged to my mother. Grandmother died there a few years later. Locked away, alone in a padded room. Forgotten. She choked on her dinner. They found her the next morning.

I'm doomed, Jem. Destined to live with a disease that robs me of my mind, makes me paranoid. To hear voices speaking from the walls, from the calendar, from your ring. To live with a stranger in my head and another in my bed. I fear that you will morph more and more into someone you are not. Into someone I think I'm already seeing.

My other choice? Take medication that strips me of all energy, sucks out any shred of motivation, of giving a damn about anything. Leaves me a drooling, jittering, quaking mass of flesh, wanting to rip my skin off and tear it to shreds. My skin turns on me, did you know that? But worst of all, I lose more and more interest in you, in sex, in love, every day. You are so beautiful, so alive. So very sexy. I never even told you that when I was in my right mind. I'm an ass, Jem. You can do better. You will do better.

Either way I look at it, I am destined to not live my life. Not the life I want. Not the life you deserve. And so I choose no medication. And I choose to save you from it all. You deserve better. Please go find it.

I love you, Jem. Sorry I waited a year before I told you. For wasting one full year as friends when I really wanted to be your lover. Be the one that you loved. But most of all I'm sorry that I loved you at all. I knew where I would end up. I shouldn't have brought you along for the ride. Not even a small part of it.

I don't know what I'm going to do now. But I wanted you to know all of this, to get it out before I lose everything. If I die, Dean will find my will. He'll know what to do. It's not what I want, death. Honestly it's not. But I fear it's where I am heading either way and I have no way of stopping it. Like a runaway train.

Love always,

Gerald.

Jem swallowed to force the bile back down her throat. Her chin trembled and her heartbeat thrummed in her ears. She folded the letter, tucked it back into the envelope, and placed it on the coffee table.

Dean put a hand on her knee. "You all right?"

She curled the ends of her closed mouth up through grit teeth

164

and tears came. She shook her head and leaned back on the sofa, her balled fists over her eyes.

"I always knew he left for me. But I thought it was my fault. Not that he wanted to save me." She sat back up and picked up the envelope. "It does answer some questions. I'm not sure what I would have done with it right after he left. I didn't know enough about his disease then. Hadn't come to terms with anything." Was still coming to terms with everything.

She stood, and he stood with her. She hugged him hard, his acrid hair product stinging her nostrils. Then two quick pats on the back and she let him go.

She watched him walk to his car, his head down, shoulders slumped. When his car turned the corner and disappeared from her sight, she shouldered the door closed, turned out the lights, and trudged up the stairs to her room on resistant feet.

In Gerald's bottom drawer, still half-full of clothes she wasn't ready to part with, his favourite sweater rested on top. She unfolded it, climbed into bed and read the letter again.

She should send a copy to Althea. No, she wouldn't send it. But she would call her. Shut that bitch up once and for all.

Jem chewed on one thumbnail while Althea's phone rang four, five, six times. Just as she was about to end the call, a clatter came through the receiver.

"What do you want, Jemima?"

"There was a will." No sense bothering with niceties. All Jem wanted to do was scream, 'I was right you stupid bitch,' into Althea's ear.

"What? You had it all along?"

"No, Dean found it. Gerald wanted to be cremated. No church. He was an atheist."

Silence except for rasping breath.

165

"He wrote me a letter too. Before he left. You want to know what he said?"

"Letters are private. You should keep it to yourself."

Like hell she would. "His father hung himself in the basement. No heart attack. Why, Althea? Why can't you just admit it? Be honest about your husband's illness? About Gerald's disease?" Tears streamed down Jem's face. The anger was gone. The hate dissipated. She no longer felt anything for this woman except pity.

Althea didn't answer. Just slammed the phone down.

That was that. The next time Jem would hear from Althea, hell would have to be filled to the rafters with winged pigs.

Jem read the letter again and again. When the sun was too low on the horizon to provide enough light, she tossed the letter on the nightstand and pulled the covers over her head. She hugged the sweater to her chest and buried her face in it. Grief that had been captive behind a barrier of so much anger, so many unanswered questions, let loose. The dam broke open and wracked her body with waves of convulsing sobs.

close that door

At the scratch of a key in the front door lock, Jem's heart leapt into her throat. She jolted up in bed, the sweater falling from her hands and onto the comforter. Footsteps padded up the staircase. She held her breath, half expecting Gerald to walk through the door.

The much taller and broader shadow of Finn crossed the entry and he stepped inside her room. "You're awake? I was trying to be quiet."

How long would it take to get used to that sound again? It'd been over a week since she had given him a key and it still made her jump.

"You succeeded. I had a rough night, that's all."

"You've been crying." He sat on the edge of the bed and ran his fingers across her cheeks.

"I must look like hell. Are my eyes swollen?" She touched her eyelids and rubbed under her eyes.

"Yes. And red." He hugged her to him and kissed her temple.

She sank into his arms. "What time is it?"

"Almost seven. Did you already go to the park?"

"No. I have no idea what time I fell asleep but it wasn't early. Do you think they'll hate me if I miss a day?"

He smiled. "I'm sure they won't. What happened? Is everything all right?"

She reached behind him and picked up the letter. "I got some answers."

He read it through in silence, pointing to a few words he couldn't make out. She translated Gerald's handwriting, something she'd done a hundred times in the past, transcribing his research notes into a digital file. Finn folded it when he was done and returned it to the night stand.

"Well, one important answer anyway. He did leave to protect you." He took her hand, brought it up to his mouth and kissed her fingers. "I'm afraid it's not going to get any easier today."

Her stomach rolled and she swallowed saliva that filled her mouth. "Why? What happened?"

He put his arm around her shoulder. "The Montreal police caught the guys who killed him."

"Are you serious?" Her mind raced, her eyes darted back and forth between his. "Who did it? Why?

"It was what we thought. A random attack. There's been a string of them there, homeless guys being beaten and robbed. They've got evidence connecting most of the incidents to these two men. That solves four attacks and two murders."

"Two random guys. One random attack. Nothing to do with Gerald at all."

"I'm afraid so."

"He died of coincidence," she whispered. Her limbs were numb, her eyes fixed on the spot on the nightstand where their photo used to sit before she hid it away. Her motives for doing that were never quite fleshed out in her head. Shame that she was sleeping with Finn in Gerald's bed and didn't want him to see? Worry that Finn would somehow be bothered by Gerald's face in her room? Or was it simply time, after forty-eight long months of being so alone, being so very lonely, that she was allowed to move on?

"So now what?" Her voice was a monotone, her mind reeled.

"They've been arraigned and are being held without bail. They face numerous charges, including murder, though they may only get manslaughter. The Crown has to prove intent for murder." He rubbed his hand up and down her arm. "Do you want to go to Montreal for the trial?"

She snapped back to reality, her heart in her throat again. "Would I have to testify?"

"No. The attack wasn't related to his disappearance. It would be more for you. Closure. Facing the people responsible."

"Of course. I knew that." She flopped back onto her pillow and rolled away from him, pulling the comforter up to her chin.

Finn lay down beside her and tucked her into the warm curve of his hard body.

She pulled his arms around her and held them close. They lay quiet for several minutes. His patience with her, their ability to just be, without the need to fill the silent emptiness with words, eased the pace of her thoughts.

"I don't want to go. I don't want to see them. It won't do me any good. And it won't do Gerald any good either."

"I understand." He kissed the back of her head and then leaned his cheek against it.

She awoke to the sound of the shower running. The clock radio showed eleven-fifteen. How easy it was to fall asleep in his arms. Damn it all to hell that it couldn't be every night.

Her cell phone rang. Althea. Bloody hell. At least Jem could give her the news. Close that door for good. If her rant from the night before hadn't already done so.

"Morning, Althea. I'm sorry about last night."

"Jem, it's Marjorie."

Jem sat up, her brow wrinkled. "Marj? Is everything all right?"

"Hon, I thought you should know. Althea passed away in the night."

"Oh no. Oh, Marjorie, I am so sorry."

"I know dear. Thank you. It was peaceful. In her sleep."

Jem doubted there was anything peaceful about it. Maybe she'd killed Althea with that phone call. "Damn, and I just learned that Gerald's murder is solved. She never got to know that."

"I'm not sure it would have helped her."

"Do you want to know the details?"

Marjorie's sigh blew through the receiver. "Maybe another day. I'm kind of full with Althea this morning. But at least that's one mystery resolved."

"Yes, one." She wasn't sure she wanted to share the rest of what she'd learned. That letter was for her and her alone and she would keep it all to herself. Except for Finn. Besides, Gerald's family already knew more than she did. It was her turn to keep a secret.

"So, Jem. How is your new man?"

"Marj, it feels kind of weird talking about that right now."

"Of course. I'm sorry, but you know me. I'm the 'get on with it' bitch. Will you come to the funeral?"

"I don't think so. We weren't the closest, you know?"

"I know. It's fine. You keep in touch, you hear me?"

"I will. Love to the family."

The day kept getting better and better.

bad, bad boy

Finn came out of the bathroom rubbing a towel through his hair, down his chest, and over his groin. "Sorry, did the shower wake you?"

How inappropriate to be turned on at a time like this.

"Yes. But it's all right, I should get moving." She stuffed both pillows behind her back and leaned into them. "I've been thinking about everything the others told him. You know what I think?"

"Not a clue."

"I think I'm them. He heard them from places in our home. Never at the office. And my grandmother's ring, that's where he spoke back. In the end, it was the only conduit between them."

"That may mean something else entirely."

"Maybe. But most of what they said was a variation on what I told him. That his mother was destined to die. That his research was too late to save her. When he spoke into the ring, was he speaking to me? Saying things his disease wouldn't let him say to the real me? I mean the weird things the others told him about how to cure cancer, that shit didn't come from me." She slid down the pillows and lay flat on the bed, pulling the comforter up to her chin. "Hell, I don't know. I need to get back to work, find some cases. Fill my brain and time with other things so I can quit obsessing over all this."

"Now that sounds like a plan." He strolled over to the bed and put his hands on either side of her body, then dove on top of her, landing as he always did, with gentle grace. His lips met hers in three quick pecks. "Is it wrong that I'm totally turned on right now?"

She pressed her head back into the pillow and laughed. "Yes. It's wicked. You're a bad, bad boy." Her arms pinned beneath the covers, she poked her head forward and kissed him, then fell back. "God, I haven't even brushed my teeth yet."

"That can wait." He tugged the sheets away.

down the rabbit hole

Jem and Finn sat down to lunch at the kitchen table. He'd made fajitas while she showered.

Gorgeous, smart, kind. And he could cook. When would she wake up from this dream?

She washed a bite of chicken and tortilla down with an icy swig of water. "Do you have the day off?"

"Afraid not." He sat forward over his plate, elbows on the table. "Should have been out of here a couple of hours ago. Can't imagine what held me up." He grinned and shoved a dripping fajita in his mouth.

"Hey, not my fault you can't control your urges." She smirked, one eyebrow raised. "Will you be back later?"

"I could be. Have to run home and do some laundry. Running low on everything."

"You could do that here."

He ate in silence for a few minutes, appearing enthralled by the contents of his plate. When he finished his last fajita he wiped his mouth and hands with a paper towel and sat back in the chair.

"I could. Maybe I could be here a lot more."

Her heart fluttered and her legs weakened. She cleared her throat. "What do you mean?"

"Maybe. No pressure. But maybe we could try living together."

"Is it too soon?" Of course it wasn't. She'd been dying to ask the same thing. Aching to wake up to his face every morning. "I mean, we've only been — together for a month."

He leaned forward, pushed their plates aside and reached across the table. He took both of her hands, picked up her paper towel and wiped salsa and fajita juice from her fingers, stealing glances at her every few seconds. He put the napkin down and brought her hands up, kissing each finger. "I've been with you for years. I'd say it's about time."

Her heart melted. "You count the time before we — as together?"

He nodded. "This last month was what I'd hoped for all along. Didn't think it would happen. But here we are."

"Yes, here we are." They stared at each other for a minute. Then she squinted at him. "You're not just looking for a better place to live, are you?"

He leaned back in the chair and held his hands up. "You got me." He winked.

"You know, I've never even been to your place. Where do you live?"

"Maybe we should stay there tonight. It is feeling a bit neglected. How about I pick you up around eight? We can get some take-out. And christen my bedroom." He flashed his eyebrows up and down.

"I guess that would be okay." She feigned disinterest, but her smile gave her away.

He leaned over the table and kissed her. "Excellent."

At eight-ten, Jem slid on her black strappy sandals with the three inch heels, smoothed the front of the fitted skirt she'd bought that afternoon, and checked her makeup and hair in the antique mirror that hung in the entry. It was only take-out at Finn's house, but it felt like a dress up date.

Five minutes later, Finn pulled up behind her van. She didn't wait for him to get to the door. She skipped down the front steps and met him halfway up the walk.

"Wow, you look great. Greater than usual."

"Thanks. Feels like a special occasion."

They shared a long kiss in the front yard for all the old fogeys to see, then he opened the passenger door of his unmarked car. "I hope you don't mind, I picked up Chinese."

Twenty minutes later they wended their way through the streets of an old and well-to-do neighbourhood. Near the top of a long, twisting drive, a left then a right, he pulled into the driveway of a huge, old sandstone house.

"Why are you stopping here?" She craned her neck forward and gaped at the house through the windshield. The building seemed to rest atop the city, basking in the glow of the setting sun. From her passenger side vantage point the view of downtown was spectacular. From the top floor of that house after dark, it would be breathtaking.

Finn put the car in park. "This is where I live."

"Excuse me? You live in this, this… mansion?"

"It's not a mansion. It's a big old house."

"In one of the oldest, richest neighbourhoods in town." She looked sideways at him and cocked her head. "Are you on the take Detective? Silk suits and castles and such?"

"Funny girl." He stepped out of the car, came around to her side and opened the door. "Come on, I'll show you around."

They climbed the many steps to the front entry. The lawn was trimmed and weed-free, the walkway framed with fuchsia and violet and cornflower and canary blooms that filled the evening air with sweet perfume.

Inside the double wooden doors with leaded glass, the old of the exterior fell away to a shining modern work of art. She gawked at the high ceiling, the winding staircase, the marble floors and massive framed paintings hanging everywhere.

Finn put one finger under her chin and closed her mouth, then put his mouth to hers. "It's not that big a deal," he said into her lips, then gave her a peck.

"That's your opinion. I feel like I fell down the rabbit hole."

He took her hand and led her through an arch into a large kitchen. Granite countertops gleamed, chrome shone, stainless stove, refrigerator, microwave, dishwasher all sparkled. Everything was spotless. Not even a fingerprint on the fridge handle.

"You spend all your time working or at my place. How the hell do you keep this place so clean? The yard so perfect?"

"I hire people for that."

One eyebrow shot up. "I beg your pardon?"

He put the bag of food on the granite island and freed dishes and chopsticks from maple cupboards. He opened the containers of noodles and ginger beef and Szechuan green beans. "My father started a fledgling oil company back in the seventies. A year later the boom hit and he expanded fast. Never looked back. It had its ups and downs, riding that industry roller coaster, but he kept it privately held. And it afforded him this." He gestured around the room.

She slid onto one of the high wooden stools that lined the other side of the island. "Amazing. So you live with your parents?"

He laughed. "No, baby. They're dead."

"Oh, I'm sorry. When?"

"They never had any luck conceiving a child. Then all of a sudden, in her forties, Mom found herself pregnant with me. She had an aneurism shortly after I was born brought on by the stress of childbirth."

"No. That's terrible. You grew up without a mother?"

"Afraid so. Had a lot of nannies. But no mother."

"What about your dad?"

"He had a stroke a few years ago. Lived in a vegetative state for a few months." Finn slid a plate of food across the granite and handed her chopsticks. "Wine?"

"Sure."

He turned to a wine rack built into the wall between two banks of cupboards and pulled a bottle from halfway up on the left. He uncorked it and popped an aerator in the top. "I should have decanted it this morning, but this works in a pinch."

She ran a finger over the smooth, cold granite slab. "You must think I'm downright backwoods."

"How so?"

"My wine doesn't even have corks."

He snickered and poured an expensive zinfandel. The burgundy liquid glugged through the aerator and into a crystal glass. No tumbler wine over ice in this house.

"Why aren't you running your dad's company? Why on earth are you a cop?"

"I was never interested in the business. It ate at him too, but he could never convince me to come on board. Since I was a kid, all I wanted was to be a policeman. Too many games of cops and robbers I guess. And I was always the cop."

"So why are you still in this house?"

"I wasn't for years. Moved out on my own at nineteen. Dad put me through college and paid my expenses until I graduated. Then I lived off my cop salary and had a small apartment downtown." He handed her a glass of wine and took a sip of his. "Then he died. Left me everything. I couldn't bring myself to sell this place. But I did sell the company. Took it public. Hold thirty-five percent of the stock. The house is paid off, the dividends alone pay for the housekeeper and gardener. And it beats the crap out of that leaky apartment with the radiator that banged all night long."

"Your wife didn't get half?"

"Not of the house or the business. I came into the marriage with that. We may have been high school sweethearts, but we didn't marry until two thousand-five." He shook his head. "Didn't realize until now that she always said no until I inherited all this. Man, I'm a blind fool."

"Love does that to you."

"Sometimes." He looked into her eyes. "And sometimes it makes you see everything with complete clarity." He leaned his elbows on the counter and raised his glass. "To what I hope is the first of many nights together under the same roof."

Come on, Jem, wake up. This couldn't be real. He couldn't be real. She pinched her thigh under the counter. Okay, that felt real.

She raised her glass and clinked it to his. "Hear, hear."

"Is that a yes? To moving in together?"

"That's a yes to talking about it. Because one of us has to give up their house." She looked around the kitchen. "And obviously it's going to be me."

"Talking about it is a fine start. There's no rush." He came around the island and put one arm around her waist, pulling her to him, then dipped his head down to hers. "I'm not going anywhere." He kissed her, long and sensual. He was in no rush at all.

After they finished eating, he took her on a tour. Behind the kitchen, the living room sprawled out across the back side of the house, the outside wall was one massive window overlooking the tops of trees and roofs of other homes. His house was the king of the castle, and the other houses were dirty rascals. A projection screen television was mounted across from chairs and sofas and loveseats that didn't match but went together. And a fireplace, floor to ceiling, slate framing its hearth, dominated one wall.

He led her through a wide hall and past a spare bedroom and spectacular guest bathroom gleaming with more granite and stainless steel. They mounted the staircase that curved from the foyer up to an open hall overlooking the entry.

"Only one room that matters right now." He swept her up into his arms and crossed through another set of double doors into a bedroom with a vaulted ceiling. He laid her on a king-size four poster bed and kissed her while he unbuttoned her blouse and stared into her eyes. "Jem?"

"Yes?"

His eyes darted back and forth, focusing on each of hers one at a time. "I've been holding something back. But I can't do this anymore."

She pushed up and rested on her elbows. "What?" Here it comes. She knew it was too good to be true. Time to wake up and get back to her real life.

He ran a hand across her cheek and through her hair then kissed her nose. He rested his forehead against hers. "I love you, Jemima. Have for years. I wanted you to know it. Know that I'm serious. That really, I'm not going anywhere. And I'm a patient man. It's all so fresh, with Gerald and all..."

She put a finger over his lips. The last thing she wanted to think about in this moment was her dead fiancé. "I love you too," she whispered.

He laughed. "Oh, thank God." Then he devoured her with an open mouth kiss.

Don't. Ever. Stop.

Jem blinked against the light piercing her eyelids. The room was awash in sunshine, the heavy drapes pulled open to the edges of the picture window. Finn's legs were entwined with hers, his arm beneath her neck. If this was a dream, then please let her never wake from it.

She shifted to her back and lifted her head. No alarm clock, but an old wooden mantle clock rested on his walnut dresser. Five-fifteen. Time to haul ass or she'd be late to the park.

In one corner of his bedroom, its footprint larger than the entire second floor of her house, an expensive, gym-worthy treadmill sat poised for use. No laundry hanging off its handles like the smaller, cheaper one in her basement. Shelves with a full set of free weights were lined up in perfect order against the wall, and a write-on/wipe-off board listed days of the week and exercises, sets and reps. He was dedicated. To everything he did. He went after what he wanted with a determined single-mindedness. In that way, he was like Gerald. But a little obsessive-compulsive disorder was the only similarity.

She glanced back at Finn, the beautiful man who now loved her. Whom she loved. Her pulse quickened, every spot on her skin where his made contact was on fire. She went to reach for his face but hesitated.

Couldn't miss two days in a row again. The residents depended on her. And she still had to get home and make sandwiches.

She slid out from under the covers and sat on the edge of the bed. The view of a sparkling downtown outside the window took her breath. Tonight she would make a point to see it in darkness. They never strayed from the bed last night, her gaze never far from his face.

The sheets rustled and Finn's lips were on her neck, one strong arm around her belly. He pulled her back into bed and curled around her from behind. "Don't go yet."

Nibbles on her shoulder and caresses to her thighs turned into a long session of early-morning lovemaking. Morning breath be damned. No shower, no problem. Nothing seemed to faze him. The smell of her own scent on his breath, the musk of his body odor, the salt of his sweat only fueled the passion, drove her further and further towards ecstasy.

It couldn't last forever. All great loves cooled at some point, fell victim to the rut of daily life. Until that happened, she'd take every second she was given. And afterwards, she'd settle into the comfort of life with Finn. If he'd have her. Even routine days with him were bound to hold more passion than the best days with Gerald.

What a traitor. At some point she needed to get past the constant comparisons and live for herself alone. For herself and Finn. Not for a dead man who'd abandoned her when she could have helped him the most.

Jem stepped out of the marble shower and wiped steam from the mirror. The same old face stared back at her but something had changed. She no longer focused on her imperfections. She'd begun to like the one crooked tooth and the golden eyes she's always thought were so weird. She combed out her hair and searched the drawers for a hairdryer. Nothing. But why would he need one? His hair was dry the second he ran a towel over it.

She wrapped a huge, soft bath towel around her and opened the door. Finn lay on his back on an exercise mat on the floor, a huge weight in each hand, his knees bent. With each push of the dumbbells skyward, he exhaled in an audible huff. Sweat glistened on his biceps, which bulged from the exercise, every sinew shown off by black athletic shorts and a tight, grey muscle-shirt.

Her cheeks flushed. It was all she could do not to jump his bones right then and there. She sidled up to him and bent over him, stared down at his face, red and dripping.

He laughed and set the weights down. "I'm not used to an audience. Makes me a bit self-conscious."

"I didn't think you had a self-conscious bone in your body."

He sat up and rubbed a towel across his face and down both arms. "I'll grab a shower then take you to get your van."

"And make sandwiches."

"We can do that here."

She cocked her head and furrowed her brow. "What, you got your own personal grocery store out back?"

"Bacon, tomato, lettuce, tuna, roast beef, cheese, bread. I got it all downstairs. Coffee's ready. I'll help with the food in five." He eyed her up and down. "And I'll get a hairdryer today so you have one here. Sorry, never thought of that."

"That would be the only thing you didn't think of." She stared at him and crossed her arms. "What the hell is the matter with you?"

His eyes widened. "Did I — are you —" He shook his head. "I'm sorry?"

"You're too perfect. There has to be something seriously wrong with you, some dastardly skeletons in the family closet. Do you gamble? Are you an alcoholic? Secretly gay?" She smiled and ran a hand over his sweaty head. "Come on, spill the beans, big fella. Don't make me go looking for it."

"You little brat. I thought you were upset with me." He reached up and tugged the towel free from her grip. He tossed it aside, grabbed her hand and pulled her to the floor.

She giggled and squirmed. "You're all sweaty."

He rolled on top of her, rubbed his body over hers and licked the side of her face. "Now you have to join me in the shower."

"I think I figured out your one big flaw."

He sucked her earlobe and shifted his body until he was between her spread legs. "Yeah? What's that?"

"You're insatiable!"

"You want me to stop?"

His erection prodded her thigh through his shorts. He bit her neck and worked his way down her body, sucking a nipple and kissing her ribs before he slid down and lifted her legs over his shoulders.

All thoughts disappeared from her mind. She closed her eyes.

The soft heat of his tongue inside of her sent waves aching through her body. He held her thighs and probed, stroked, sucked.

Her back arched, fingers dug into the mat. An orgasm released loud groans from deep in her chest. She eased her grip on the mat, her breath coming fast and shallow.

He kissed her thighs, her belly, her breasts, her neck, and made his way up to her face.

She stared into his mischievous eyes. "No, don't stop. Don't. Ever. Stop." She brought up her legs, gripped the waistband of his shorts with her toes and tugged them down.

They set up an assembly line along the granite island. Finn spread mustard and mayo on bread. Jem added meat, tomato, and cheese. When enough sandwiches were prepared, they wrapped them with parchment and packed them into boxes alongside fruit and juice.

He'd thought of everything.

"I almost forgot." He opened the fridge and pulled two Oh! Henry's from the butter keeper in the door. "For Joe."

Most thoughtful man ever.

"Thank you. I hope he can put on some weight." She tucked the bars into a box. "Any word from the Regina police?"

"Anders has been calling twice a day. It doesn't seem to be a priority for them. I'll check in with her and let you know." He slid behind her, kissed her cheek, and hugged her to him on the way by. "In the meantime." He pulled a small box from a drawer under the wine rack. "I have something to return to you." He placed the box in her hand.

She glanced up at him and opened the lid. Inside, nestled in a bed of cotton fluff, clean and sparkling, her grandmother's ring glinted in the morning sunlight. Her breath caught in her throat.

"I can have it back?"

"Not evidence anymore. It's all yours."

He plucked the ring from the box and took her left hand.

Her heart leapt. Gerald's engagement ring may as well have been a flashing neon light. Look, Finn, it said. I haven't let go yet. I'm hanging on to a ghost.

He hesitated. "Where do you wear it?"

She held up her right hand and wiggled the ring finger.

He smiled. "Right. Of course." He slid it on. "Seems kind of big."

"I might have lost some weight. Probably this new sexercise regimen you've got me on." She moved the ring to her middle finger. "There, that works."

Jem and Finn stood at the side door to her van and necked in the morning sunshine. Finn was late for work, but he didn't seem to care.

He pulled away from her and wiggled his eyebrows. "My place or yours?"

She put both of her palms flat against his chest. "Let's play it by ear. How late will you be?"

"Should be before seven. But you never know. Sorry, I can't make any promises."

"I know. That's fine. Text me later?"

"Definitely."

She waved when he pulled away from the curb and watched him until he turned right at the stop sign. She shut the van and ran into the house, swapped her high heels and snug skirt for flip flops and walking shorts. The reflection of the pearl ring in the mirror made her hesitate. It had been years since she'd seen it, years since she'd worn it. It was beautiful, but clunky and awkward. And she saw Gerald's face whenever she looked at the pearl.

She yanked it off her finger and tucked it in beneath her underwear, slammed the drawer and raced out of the house.

When she pulled up to the park, her regular spot was taken. It took two trips around the block before she found an opening.

"Ruby, you're late, love. We were worried about you. Where you been?"

"Sorry guys. I didn't feel well yesterday. And I might start coming a little later from now on. I never have to go to the office anymore, so I can make my own hours." And she could think of no good reason to maintain Gerald's old time schedule.

Frank and Angus shared a look.

"You okay, Jem?" Frank cocked his head to one side, his eyebrows knit. "You didn't lose your job or nothing did you?"

"Didn't lose it. Chose to leave. Going to open my own law practice."

Angus slapped her on the shoulder. "Good for you. Work for your own benefit, not some asshole big shot in the corner office. No boss? No problem."

"You got it. And if you two ever need a lawyer, I'd never charge you a cent."

"That's mighty generous of you." Frank nodded. "But we never needed a lawyer before."

"Good to hear."

She made her way around the park, handed out food, and let the residents all know the change of time. Last stop was Joe.

"Hey, Joe. How is today treating you?"

He shrugged and took the offered food.

"Here, two Oh! Henry's. To make up for missing yesterday. Courtesy of my boyfriend."

He smiled and nodded. "Thanks." His voice was stronger than before. Like he'd been using it in her absence.

"You're welcome. I'll tell him you said so."

She let him finish his breakfast and gathered up his garbage as had become their custom. She'd decided on the drive to the park that it was time to push for details. Time to figure out who this man was and what horrible event had scarred him, physically and mentally. Time to help him heal.

She cleared her throat. "Joe?" It came out as a mere whisper. Her heart pounded. She cocked her head to one side and looked him in the eye. "Are you Joseph Carlisle?"

He froze. Sweat beaded on his brow. His gaze darted all around the park and then he shifted sideways. He was going to bolt.

"No, Joe. Don't leave. It's all right." She put a hand on his arm and patted it.

He settled back down. His eyes filled with tears. "How?"

"I checked into missing persons cases. Someone in Regina is

looking for you Joe. Who is it?"

He shook his head. "No one."

"If it was no one, you wouldn't be in the database. Do you remember what happened?" She touched the scar above his eye. "How this happened?"

He turned his head. "Yes."

"Do you want to tell me about it?"

"No."

"Okay. I understand." She looked around the park. "Well, no I don't understand. But it's none of my damn business." She took the second sandwich and handed it to him. "I'm sorry for intruding, Joe. I worry for you. I want you to get your life back. You don't belong here."

How could she breach the walls he'd built? Not mere baby steps — she wanted a jump-over-the-cliff, leap-before-you-look, honest-to-goodness breakthrough.

"Joe, if you want to talk to someone, the shelter has people willing to listen. They know their stuff. And you would be in control. Tell them as much or as little as you choose. Stop any time."

He crossed his arms. "Maybe."

"Okay. That's better than no." She stood and brushed grass from her backside. "Will you be here tomorrow?"

He stared at the sandwich, his shoulders slumped. Then he shrugged. "Yeah."

"Will you let me help you?"

He looked up at her and sighed. "I don't know."

"Good enough for now. See you tomorrow."

whatever it takes

Jem tossed empty boxes down the basement steps. She sat on a towel on the bare cement and pulled medical journals and reference manuals from Gerald's shelves. She filled one box destined for Dean's office at the university. Dust floated in a ray of sun that streamed in through the small window above the washing machine. A tingle built up in her chest, and a loud sneeze broke the silence.

She tried to lift the box. Nothing doing. She set her jaw, put her shoulder to the box and pushed. It didn't budge."God damn it!" She kicked the box. "Shit, shit, shit." She kicked it with each curse, every blow an exorcism of the anger and frustration and hurt that she wanted to unleash on Gerald. She kicked it until a small hole broke open and her big toe throbbed.

Arms across her chest, she stood back and surveyed the damage. "Stupid idiot," she said aloud. Where was the duct tape?

Would it be weird to ask Finn to help her take it out to the van? Yes, it would. She sent Dean a text asking when he'd like to pick it up.

She pitched winter boots, scarves and gloves into a second box. Her defiance of all Gerald's order and exactitude was complete when that box stood full, a jumbled, unfolded confusion of disorder. Another empty box stood at her feet, ready for its open maw to be filled with another cluttered pile of his belongings.

She stood in front of the clothes rack in the basement. She always loathed the semi-annual chore of swapping warm-weather jackets and shoes for winter gear. That was one thing she and Gerald both disliked about their little house. The little closets.

She grasped the hanger that held his heavy faux-sheepskin coat, still in the plastic from its last annual spring trip to the dry cleaner four years ago. She lifted it from the rack. Its weight surprised her and pulled her arm straight down. The coat landed on the floor. How did he ever haul this thing around on his spare frame? She shed the plastic, rolled the coat and crammed it into the box on top of the other winter wear.

Two hours later, seven boxes were packed and sealed. Some for Dean, some for the shelter, and some for the dump. The basement should be empty, but it was still cluttered with five years of their mixed lives, and four of her solitary one.

She needed more boxes.

Her cell phone rang. She ran up the stairs and snatched it from the kitchen table. "Hello?"

"You're out of breath. Everything okay?"

Every fiber of her body relaxed at the sound of Finn's deep voice. His presence, the mere thought of him, the smell of his skin. That was where she lived now. Where she needed to be. "Yeah, had to run up the stairs to get the phone. Out of shape I guess."

"I have to come over. Now."

"Insatiable." She drew out the syllables in a sing-song voice and leaned one shoulder against the wall.

"No, not that. I have some information. About Joseph."

She straightened. "What? Tell me."

"I have to show you in person. It's a lot."

"All right. So hurry up."

She ended the call and turned to head back downstairs. Gerald's write-on/wipe-off calendar stopped her in her tracks. Before she could second-guess the decision, she peeled the laminated sheet from the wall. Years-old double-sided tape pulled paint and a layer of drywall with it. She rolled the calendar into a tight cylinder and bent it over her knee, like she was breaking a stick. She shoved the calendar into the garbage bin, pushed it down as far as it would go. When she pulled her hand out of the bin, her engagement ring slid past her knuckles. She made a fist before it slipped from her finger and into the trash.

She really had lost weight. She took the ring off and held it up to the light, then held out her ring-free left hand. A white band of skin remained, indented where the gold band had lived for six years. She shook her head. Why had she kept herself shackled to a dead man?

A car pulled up out front and the engine cut. She peered out through the sheer drape of the front door. Finn. She slipped the ring into the front pocket of her shorts and opened the door.

Finn climbed the stairs, a file in his hand. "Regina finally got back to Anders." He brushed past her and headed straight for the kitchen.

"Whoa, not even a hello?"

Finn spilled papers and photos out of the manila folder and onto the table. "Hello," he said, one eyebrow lifted. He sifted through the mess and pulled out a photo. "You want to see the details?"

She crossed her arms. "I don't know what the details are yet."

"Sorry." He took a deep breath and handed her the eight-by-ten photo.

A crumpled SUV, shattered glass, a light standard where the engine should be. The passenger side was crushed, airbags deployed and lying flaccid amid the wreckage. Glass and airbags were stained crimson.

"What is this?"

"Joseph's vehicle. After the accident."

She gasped, her gaze shifted from the picture to Finn. "How did he survive?"

"The passenger side took the worst of it. He was cut up pretty bad, concussion. Could have been worse. Should have been worse." He sifted through the papers and pulled out another picture.

Joe sat on a hospital gurney. His eyes, dull and vacant, stared past the camera. Blood from a deep gash above his right eye covered most of his face and stained the front of his shirt. His arms were a roadmap of cuts and slashes.

"I've seen those scars. But what does the accident have to do with him being in the park?"

Finn retrieved another photo from the table. "This is his wife."

She took the photo, her eyes locked on Finn's. Two deep breaths and she shifted her gaze to the picture. Her knees went weak and nausea rolled up her throat. "Oh, shit."

Finn took the picture and turned it face down on the table. "She was crushed. Most of her bones shattered. Joe managed to get free of the wreckage and tried to pull her out the broken window, tried to rescue her. It wouldn't have mattered if he'd succeeded, she wouldn't have made it. Fire and rescue used the Jaws of Life to cut her out." He shifted on his feet and reached for Jem's hand. "She never regained consciousness. Joe watched her die in the ICU."

"Oh, poor Joe." Tears streamed down her cheeks.

"It was the hospital that reported him missing."

"The hospital?"

"After she died he went mute. He wouldn't speak. He just left. Slipped out without anyone noticing. No one's seen him since."

"But why does the hospital care where he is? Why hasn't family come forward?"

"Only child, parents both dead." He flipped through pages held in a file with a metal clip. "No close relatives, only distant cousins who didn't even know he was missing." He tossed the file onto the table. "Jem, she was pregnant. Full term."

"He lost his wife and child at one time? No wonder he doesn't care if he's found."

"No, that's not it. You see, he doesn't know." He glanced at the ceiling and emptied his lungs. "Jem, he has a daughter. They saved the baby."

"Oh my God. Oh my God." She shook her hands and paced the floor, then wheeled around. "We have to tell him. He needs to know."

"Yes. But we need to take this slow. That news could send him into shock."

"Yes, yes. Of course. I should call Sid. Get a professional to help with this." Her eyes darted around the room, her mind raced, she paced the floor. Then she stopped short and looked at Finn. "When did this all happen? How old is she?"

"It was November last year. She's barely eight months old."

She nodded. "November. That's when Joe went missing." The baby would be too young to remember, to be scarred by the separation from a father she'd never met. "Where is she?"

"Well, here's where it gets complicated." He sat at the table. "His brother-in-law, his wife's brother, has been given temporary custody of the baby. He's filed for adoption based on the assumption of parental abandonment."

"Abandonment? Joe never would have left if he'd known."

"Exactly. And a full year has to pass for a court to agree to classify it as abandonment. I'm sure there's more to this, but that's all we have right now. Anders had no luck contacting the brother-in-law."

"I'll call him. I'm Joe's attorney."

"This guy might think Joe is dead. Or insane. Either way, a call out of the blue from his lawyer might not be the best plan. Especially since Joe doesn't even know you're officially representing him."

She propped her right elbow in her left palm and chewed on her thumbnail. "He needs that little girl." She paced into the living room and back. "What's her name?"

"Emma Jean. After her mother."

"I want to see her."

"Jem, I can't give you their address."

"If I'm his lawyer, fighting for custody of his natural born child, don't you have to?"

Finn sighed. "Maybe. But that might be quite the fight. He did leave. He is clearly not in his right mind."

"If his brother-in-law knows he's here, if we get him help… Hell, if he knows that child is alive, I'm sure Joe will come around. He'll do whatever it takes."

"How do you know that?"

She slumped into a chair. "I just do."

don't sell the house

Jem wanted to blurt out to Joe that he had a daughter. Give him something to hold on to. Some reason to jump back into life. She couldn't bring herself to make eye contact with him, afraid the secret might be visible in her gaze.

But Finn was right. Mentioning his last name almost sent him running. If he learned he'd abandoned a child he thought he was responsible for killing, he may end up catatonic. One step at a time. There was no way to ease into that conversation.

She gathered his refuse and balled it up in her hands. "So, Joe. I'm going to be pushy today, okay?"

His brow creased.

"What did you do in Regina? For a living I mean." He was a school teacher. She knew that. It was so dishonest, asking him things she knew the answers to. But this situation required unconventional, or underhanded, means. "Were you a lawyer, like me?"

He made a face and shook his head.

"Hey now. We're not all bad."

He smiled.

"A doctor?"

Head shake.

"Come on, give me a hint."

"Teacher."

"Ooh, good hint." She tapped her index finger on her cheek. "Let's see. Were you a teacher?"

He laughed. An actual out loud snicker.

"High school?"

Head shake.

"Junior high?"

Nod.

"Okay. Junior high school teacher. Science?"

"Math."

"Yuck. My least favourite."

He smiled.

"Do you miss it? Your students, the school?"

He stared at the ground and nodded.

"Why don't you go back?"

He shook his head. "Not yet."

Yet? That was a first. A possibility. An opening.

"Joe, I can help. If you need money. If you need me to contact anyone." She put a hand on his knee. "Would you please speak to a therapist? Someone who can help you work through whatever it is that is keeping you here?"

He pulled at tufts of grass. Then he looked her in the eye. "Maybe. Maybe."

"All right. That's great. I'll let you think about that. Can we talk more tomorrow?"

He nodded.

"I'm going to be pushy again, you okay with that?"

He smiled. One nod. "Thank you."

"My pleasure."

The front door creaked. Jem turned away from the fry pan to appreciate the sight of Finn as he entered the kitchen and slipped his suit jacket over the back of a chair. He pulled his tie loose and met her at the stove for a kiss.

"Mm, fried onions. What are you making?"

"Perogies. Not making them. Boiling the frozen ones."

"Oh, so disappointed you don't stuff your own." He grinned at her and she pretended to slap him with the greasy wooden spoon.

They scooped dumplings onto their plates and smothered them in sour cream, bacon and onions. Jem filled two glasses with wine and sat across from him. Each time he crossed her threshold she was struck by how happy she was. Finn's presence in her life was lifting the Gerald fog. The crazy, the distance, the disappearance. For years it had dominated her life. And now it was gone, over, closed. She began to see joy again, to relax and be herself. To just be.

She cut a dumpling in half with the side of her fork. "Joe said he might see a therapist."

"That's great. You didn't tell him —"

"No. Not yet. But I want to. Soon. He's missed so much already. Tomorrow I want to ask about the accident. Somehow. Without him knowing what I know."

"I'm beginning to think you should tell him what you know."

"Believe me, I'm dying to. But I'm afraid I'll lose his trust. If I lose that I'll lose him altogether."

"I suppose." He stood, took her empty plate and set it in the sink with his. He turned and leaned against the cupboard, his arms crossed. "Have you put any more thought into us living together? Not to pressure you or anything, but can we talk about it?"

"Other than Joe, I've thought about nothing else." She crossed the floor and tucked her hands between his arms and body until he uncrossed his arms and hugged her. "I want to. I mean, I really, really want to. It sounds perfect." She cocked her head to one side and looked around her kitchen. "It's the house. I'd have to give up the house. It used to be 'our' place, you know? But in the last couple of years it became mine. I kept it up for four years, made payments, handled it all alone. I want you to know that's why it's hard to give up, not because of Gerald."

His face softened. "Jem I don't ever want you to forget Gerald. Or give up the things that represented him in your life. I've kept mementos of my relationship, my marriage. That's normal." He squeezed her to him. "I'm not jealous of your feelings for Gerald. I hope you wouldn't be jealous of mine for Amy. They're only memories, not here-and-now realities."

"Seriously," she whispered. "What is wrong with you? Because I can't find anything."

He pulled away and leaned against the counter, his arms crossed in front of his chest. He sighed. "I work hard to be different than I used to be."

"How did you used to be?"

"Angry."

"I can't imagine that."

"I've see a lot of shit in this job. My father's death left me pretty messed up. I was an adult but suddenly I felt like an orphaned child. And my marriage, the direction it took, made me pretty bitter. Amy was tough to live with. But I was impossible."

"Wow. Way to sell me on living with you." She grinned.

"I see a therapist twice a month. I've turned the anger around and have been able to focus that negative energy into more positive outcomes." He took one of her hands. "I'll tell you what's wrong with me now. I'm obsessive. I obsess over work. Obsessed over your case, over you. That was the last straw that finally blew my marriage apart. I obsess over exercise and fitness. And now," he tickled her ribs, "I'm obsessed with getting you to live with me."

She giggled and pushed his hand away. "Don't forget sex. You're obsessed with sex."

"Only with you." He brushed her hair aside and took her earlobe in his mouth. His teeth scraped against her skin and his tongue left a moist trail from her ear to her neck. He slid his hand inside her shirt at the shoulder and slipped it down her arm. Firm bites and feather kisses followed the path of his hand until her fastened buttons prevented him going any further. With his other hand he undid them one by one, moving his lips closer to her elbow with each popped button.

She shut her eyes and let the sensation of his tongue and his teeth on her skin melt the rest of the world away. No matter how often he held her, kissed her, made love to her, her chest ached and she went weak in the knees.

He took her hand and led her to the living room, drew the curtains shut and undressed her, kissing and tasting every inch of her skin as it was uncovered. She pulled his shirt free of his waistband and pulled it over his head. He stood, dropped his pants and kicked them towards the front entry.

She fanned the fingers of her right hand over his chest and pushed. He dropped backwards onto the sofa. She straddled him, her hands on his shoulders, and rocked with him inside her, his face buried between her breasts.

She was on the verge of climax when he held her still and kissed her. Then he wrapped his arms around her and picked her up. He set her feet on the floor, turned her away from him and bent her over the wide armrest of the chair. He bent with her, his chest pressing against her back, one arm around her middle. His lips and tongue danced on her neck. Quakes of pleasure shot through her body.

Of all the men she'd been with, none had the strength to manipulate her body, position her anywhere and everywhere without a word, and with such gentle ease. She was safe in his hands. Safe with him. In every way imaginable.

He brought her to the brink of climax again and then slowed. "Damn," he whispered in her ear. "Let me run upstairs and get a condom."

She reached one hand behind his head. "No. Don't stop."

With that slight encouragement he kept going until they were both moaning and panting. They climaxed together and he went limp against her back. He grabbed her, spun around, and fell over the armrest into the chair, pulling her down on top of him. He hugged her and nuzzled his face into her neck.

"That was amazing. Wish we could do it bare every time."

"We can."

"Jem, I love you but I'm not ready to be a father."

She twisted her neck around and looked at him. "I went on the pill two weeks ago."

He stared at her and ran a hand through her hair. He brought his lips to hers and they shared another kiss. "Perfect," he whispered.

They sat in the chair in silence for several minutes, their naked bodies curled up against each other. Her head rested against his shoulder, her nose buried beneath his chin.

"I have an idea." He kissed her forehead. "Only a suggestion. Something to think on."

"Shoot."

"Don't sell your house. Keep it."

She shifted and looked up at him. "You want to give up your mansion and cram in here with me?"

"That wouldn't be a bad thing — as long as we're under the same roof. But I was thinking you could move in with me and turn your house into an office. Run your practice out of it."

She settled back onto his shoulder. One finger stroked little circles on his chest. The best of both worlds. Live in a mansion with this god of a man. Keep her house as a place of business. And have a fall-back home in case things went south with Finn. Not that they would, but a girl's got to be practical. "I did buy a desk from Ikea. Almost got it together in the spare room but gave up."

"The living room could be a meeting place. The kitchen could be your office — handy to the coffee machine and all. And you could keep your bedroom as a bedroom. You know, for when I drop in some afternoons for a quickie." He tickled her ribs.

She giggled. "You've really thought this through."

She glanced around the room. What was she holding on to? It was only a house, just plywood and plaster. Keeping it wouldn't bring Gerald home, wouldn't turn back time. It didn't even hold all the best memories of him. The more often she replayed their short time here, the more the truth started to smack her upside the head. The house represented Gerald's worst.

"I like that idea," she whispered. The feel of Finn's warm skin against hers, the touch of his hand, his soft kiss. That was home. She didn't want to be alone anymore. To be lonely. No way would she let this go sideways.

"Yes."

He sat up and looked her in the eye, his smile bright, his face lit up. "Really?"

"Really."

He slid out from under her, stood and pulled her to her feet. In one quick movement she was up and over his shoulder, her bare ass right next to his face. He tapped it in a playful spank. "Let's go celebrate."

He jogged up the stairs to her room and tossed her on the bed. She bounced on the mattress and he dove on top of her.

Insatiable.

acknowledgement of her existence

"Good morning, Joe." Jem dropped to the grass and crossed her legs.

Joe lifted one hand in a wave.

"Pastrami on rye, bananas, and orange juice today."

"Mustard?"

"What else?"

He dug into his breakfast and smiled.

"You're in a good mood today. Did you shave again?" She ran the back of her fingers along his cheek. Clean with a hint of stubble.

He nodded and swallowed pastrami. "Showered at the shelter last night."

Butterflies danced in her stomach. That was the first full sentence he'd ever spoken to her. His voice was strong, his eyes bright. "That — that's wonderful. Did you sleep there too?"

"Yeah. More comfortable."

"I bet." She leaned back on her palms and looked skyward. The sun sparkled behind the leaves of tall trees. A slight breeze shifted branches, the sun playing peek-a-boo behind the foliage. "What a beautiful day."

"Yes. Warm." He finished the last bite of his sandwich, peeled the banana, and stared at the ground. "I talked to someone."

She bolted upright. "Excuse me?"

"At the shelter. A counselor."

"Joe, that's wonderful. Fantastic. How do you feel about it?"

"Pretty good. Good to talk. To cry."

"And now what?"

"Going back. He's lost people. Left people."

"And he got his life back?"

He nodded.

"Joe, do you want your life back?"

"Won't be the same. But maybe."

Inside her head she screamed and jumped up and down and danced a little jig. But she showed him a serious face. "Who did you leave behind, Joe? In your old life?"

"No one."

"What about your wife. I know you have one. The ring, remember?"

His face reddened and tears fell. "Emma."

Her heart skipped a beat. There it was. Acknowledgment of her existence.

"That's a lovely name." She sat forward and looked him in the eye "Where is Emma, Joe? Are you divorced?"

He shook his head and wiped his cheeks and nose, rubbed the back of his hand on his filthy pants.

She reached towards him touched the scars on his arm. "Joe, what happened? Please tell me."

"Car accident."

"Is that how you got your scars?"

He nodded "My fault. She died."

Tears sprung to Jem's eyes. "I'm so sorry, Joe." She held his hand and let the weight of the moment rest. "Joe?" she whispered. "How was it your fault?"

His eyes flashed. Not anger. Not at her. "I was driving. Lost control." He hung his head, covered his face with his hands and sobbed. "I tried to save her."

"Okay, okay. I'm sorry. No more questions today. But here's something for you to consider." She stroked his head. "Not all accidents are someone's fault. Sometimes they are circumstances beyond your control. Let's work on letting you forgive yourself, okay? Maybe talk to the counselor about forgiveness. Do you think you can do that?"

He glared at her. "I doubt it."

"All right. You're in control. Would you consider seeing a psychologist?"

"I have no money."

"If money wasn't a concern, and you could get therapy, real therapy — would you?"

"I suppose. But no money."

"I know someone. You wouldn't have to pay him. Can I take you to him?"

He rested his hands in his lap and looked across the park. "Maybe," he whispered.

leap right through

Jem carried the last box of her clothes down the stairs and stacked it with the others in the living room. She ran a hand over the back of the chair and eyed the sofa. Finn's house was jam-packed with furniture, all of it newer and nicer than anything she owned. Perhaps a charity would like her living room set and the television, so tiny compared to Finn's projection screen.

She sat on the sofa, grabbed a throw cushion and hugged it to her chest. She closed her eyes and remembered the day she and Gerald had picked out the furniture. Neither had anything worth bringing into a new home, so they decided to donate their old stuff and start fresh with things that belonged to the two of them.

Now she was giving it up and accepting that she'd live with things that were Finn's and Finn's alone. Or Finn's and Amy's.

She glanced around the room. Her gaze paused on the hole behind the television where Gerald had ripped the cable from the wall, on the shelves now vacant of Gerald's awards and photos. She'd spent so many nights and weekends alone even before they moved in together, waiting for Gerald to stop working, to stop writing, to stop long enough to pay her any attention at all.

She'd wanted a soft sofa and comfortable chairs that reclined. He thought they were gauche. Pedestrian. He wanted something nice, classy. With legs you could vacuum under and deep-but-sturdy cushions and high armrests. Something you'd be proud to show off when you had guests, he'd said. Even though they never had guests. And he rarely used the living room furniture.

None of this was hers. It was his. All his. She'd lost every argument, every discussion. Not because he was completely rigid. No, it was her fault. She always caved in to what he wanted. Funny how that reality dimmed over the years and some legend of him, of their relationship, took its place. No, she didn't need any of this. It could all go.

The lock clicked and the door popped open. Finn's head appeared from behind the door. "Hey, you all packed?"

"Kind of. All my clothes and bathroom stuff."

"I can get a moving van this weekend. We can put all this furniture downstairs. I always wanted to make a family room down there. Never had a good reason to."

"I like the idea of a family room, but not with this stuff. I'm letting it all go. We can figure out the basement later. Maybe with stuff for us."

He crossed the floor and sat beside her, wrapped his arm around her shoulder and pulled her against him. "For us. I like it." He kissed her temple. "If there's anything in the house that you don't want, don't like. Just say so."

"Your home is beautiful."

"Our home. And I'm serious. Anything. You tell me, promise?"

"Promise." She licked her lips. "There is one thing. It's stupid, really."

"I doubt that. What is it?"

"In your living room. The sculpture."

He smiled. "The abstract. Bodies entwined."

"That's the one."

"It isn't about me and Amy." He kissed her forehead. "I bought that last month."

She pulled away and looked at his face. "Before we — or after?"

"A couple of days after."

She gazed into his eyes. "Then it can stay."

"All right then. Let me load these boxes up. I've got champagne in the fridge. I think a night in is in order, no?"

She smiled and tossed the cushion aside. "My favourite. Maybe we can imitate the sculpture."

"I can get on board with that." They shared a brief kiss. He stood and grabbed two boxes at a time and jostled through the doorway.

She ran her hands over the seat of the sofa, sighed, stood and picked up a box. Her eyes surveyed the small space one last time before stepping outside.

She was keeping the house. Would be there almost every day for her practice. But it wouldn't be Gerald's house. Not their house. No, she'd closed the door on that chapter of her life. And was about to swing a new one wide open and leap right through.

Finn placed a dress on a padded hanger and tucked it into the empty side of his closet. Her side. "I spoke with the Regina police this afternoon."

"And?"

"I confirmed that Joseph has been found here. Not sure where to go from there. He's a grown man. They can't force him to go home. But if he doesn't, then his brother-in-law's bid for custody will be a no-brainer. It'll be ruled parental abandonment."

She sat on the floor in front of Finn's massive walnut dresser, refolded tank tops and sweaters, and placed them into the drawers Finn had cleaned out for her. "We have to tell him. If he knows about his daughter, he'll go back."

"They asked me to join them when they interview the brother-in-law. I'm going tomorrow."

She perked up. "And me."

"I didn't figure I'd get away without you. I told them you represent Joe. Already got you a plane ticket."

She smiled. Of course he did. "Thanks. Getting him his parental rights back is my first official case. Even if my client doesn't know it yet."

"What's your first move, legally speaking?"

"I've got to make a few calls. It's not my usual area. But I have some contacts. I'm hoping Sid will see him, get him some preliminary therapy. Not sure if that's going to be necessary, but I'm betting so. And I'll pay you back for the ticket."

He pulled her up from the floor. "It's on me. Consider it an office-warming gift."

She tucked her fingers into the waistband of his pants and tugged him towards her. "As long as it's not for services rendered." She stood on her tiptoes and crushed her lips to his.

Jem lounged sideways across an oversize chair in the living room of her new home. Her legs thrown over one armrest, she ran her hand across the leather and stared out at the tops of the birch and aspen that grew in the yards of the houses below. The view was perfect. The house was perfect. Finn was perfect. How did this happen to her?

She eyed the spotless room. At least she'd never have to dust or vacuum again. That was perfect too.

She plucked her cell phone from her stomach and punched numbers in. She gnawed on her thumbnail. Four, five, six rings. Damn it, pick up.

"Hello, Jemima."

"Sid, hi. Look, do you remember that homeless man I told you about?"

"Yes, you thought PTSD, right?"

"Right. Would you see him? He can't pay. If you don't want to do it for free, I can foot the bill. I've made progress and I don't want to let it backslide."

"All right. Can you bring him tomorrow afternoon? Say four-thirty?"

"No, not tomorrow. We've found out who he is, and he has a daughter he thought died — a baby. I haven't told him yet. Not sure how I'm going to. But tomorrow I'm going to Regina to see her and to speak with the uncle who's been taking care of her. We're back same day, how about the day after?"

"Sure, let's see." Paper rustled through the receiver. "How about the morning. Ten?"

"That's perfect. If we don't show up it's because I couldn't get him to come. But I have a feeling he will."

"See you then. But Jemima, you might want me to tell him about his daughter. In the office, in a controlled environment."

Not bloody likely. She wanted to be the bearer of that particular good news. "Thanks, Sid. You're a peach."

not your child

Jem sat in the window seat of the Boeing 737. Finn was stuffed into the small space beside her, his knees jammed against the seat in front, his shoulder and arm infiltrating her space.

In the stale air of the cabin, her chest heaved. The spout above her head offered a thin stream of cold air that blew her bangs into her eyes and tickled the fine hairs on her cheek. She reached up and twisted it shut. Within two minutes, her body overheated. She squirmed and wrested her arms free from the summer-weight black suit jacket with the three-quarter sleeves. The smell of sweat and other people's feet overtook the air around her. The constant loud hum of the engine made her head throb. She turned the air conditioning spout back on and aimed it away from her face.

Finn touched her bare forearm. She started and jerked it away.

"Jumpy much?" His quizzical eyebrow taunted her.

"Sorry. But yes. I almost feel guilty that we get to meet his daughter before he does."

The flight attendant rolled an aluminum cart down the aisle, bumping Finn's elbow when she came to a stop beside him.

Jem passed on the meager snack offerings but accepted a cup of coffee. She sipped it, wrinkled her nose at the strong, distasteful brew and shifted in her seat.

Finn flipped through the growing number of pages in Joseph's file. "Man, he's only twenty-four."

"Joe? That can't be right."

"No, his brother-in-law, Bill Engles. And single. That's a lot to take on, raising someone else's child, even in better circumstances."

The intercom scratched to life and announced the slow descent into Regina. Jem stared out the window at the city below. Joe's brother-in-law shouldn't be strapped with his dead sister's baby. He should be finding his own life. Falling in love and having his own children.

When the plane stopped a hundred yards from the terminal and the seatbelt light went out, Finn unbuckled and stood. He shook his legs and bent them a few times.

"Too cramped?"

"Always. Too bad this flight has no first class seats."

He stepped back and held Jem's hand while she squeezed from the seat. Outside the porthole, a staircase rolled towards the plane. A few bangs and grinds later and the door opened. They stepped out into a windy, overcast day and made their way down the steps and across the tarmac. Waiting near the terminal doors, was one uniformed officer and a man in a suit with 'cop' written all over him. He stepped towards Finn.

"Detective Wight?"

Finn held out his hand. "Jefferson? Nice to meet you." They shared a stiff handshake, just one manly pump of the arm. Finn put a hand on the small of Jem's back. "This is Joseph Carlisle's lawyer, Jemima Stone."

"Pleasure, ma'am."

"Jem, thanks. Ma'am really isn't my style."

The car headed north from the airport. A few minutes, and several turns, later they were whipping along a country road at a good clip.

Jem stared out the car window and watched miles of wheat and crops speed by while the endless horizon held its place in the distance. Good thing they flew in. If she'd had to drive through this flat nothingness she'd have nodded off at the wheel and hit the ditch for sure.

After fifteen minutes, they turned into a gravel laneway and pulled up in front of a Victorian-style farm house. Gravel crunched under the tires of Jefferson's unmarked cruiser as it rolled to a stop. Jem stepped from the back seat and surveyed the acreage.

Mature trees of all varieties surrounded the front yard. From a thick branch of one maple, a tire swing hung, the rubber faded from exposure to the elements, chains spotted with rust. Next to it, a child's plastic swing swayed in the breeze. It was the baby kind, white and blue and orange, with leg holes and a chest restraint. It dangled from thick rope. No chains for tiny fingers to get caught in. It looked brand new next to the old tire.

She followed Finn and Jefferson up four wooden steps onto a wide porch that wrapped around the house. The space was shaded and protected by the floors of the rooms overhead. Next to a large picture window, a wooden porch swing hung from the ceiling, a smattering of large building blocks littered the floor in front of it. A rag doll sat slumped over in the swing.

Jefferson rapped his knuckles on the door, three sharp knocks. From inside, footsteps neared the entry, then the curtain was pulled aside. A young man peered out at them, his hair mussed, eyes sleepy.

"Mr. Engles?" Jefferson flashed his badge at the window. "Can we speak to you? It's about your brother-in-law, Joseph Carlisle."

The door creaked open and Bill Engles stepped onto the porch. "What about him? You find his body or something?"

Jem drew back, her mouth dropped open. Was this man made of

steel?

"No sir." Jefferson pulled at his tie. "He's been found. Alive. In Calgary."

"What? Who found him?"

"I did." Jem held her hand up, fingers splayed.

"How'd you even know he was missing?"

"I didn't. He showed up one day, in a park where I go most mornings. I started talking to him, trying to get him to talk to me. He hasn't said much."

From inside the open door, a baby cried. Bill excused himself and slipped into the house. He returned with a small girl in his arms. Her blonde curls were messed from sleep. She yawned and rubbed her eyes. Red-rimmed steel grey eyes.

Jem's heart skipped a beat. The child was a ringer for Joe. A ringer with fat cheeks and soft, feathery, never-cut hair. A ringer who smelled of baby powder and Arrowroot biscuits instead of months old body odour and filth. "Is this Emma?"

"Yes. Emma Jean Engles."

"You mean Carlisle."

"Maybe legally. For now. But when I adopt her it'll be Engles."

"Mr. Engles, you don't understand." She glanced at Finn and Jefferson, waiting for one of them to stop her, but no one did. "Joseph has been found. He's her father." She eyed the way he held the girl, both arms engulfing her, protecting her from being snatched away. She squinted. "Did you even try to look for him?"

"No. Why should I? He up and left his kid alone."

"But he didn't know she'd survived. He'd just watch his wife die —"

"My sister."

"Yes. Your sister. I'm so sorry for your loss. But Joe thought the baby died too. He was distraught. In shock. He still is."

"I don't care. It's his fault anyway. He caused that accident. He killed my sister. Why should he even get to see Emma?"

Finn stiffened. "Mr. Engles, I'm afraid you've got some bad information there."

Bill shifted his attention to Finn, his brow furrowed. "He lost control, slammed into a light pole. How can that not be his fault?"

"It was no one's fault. The roads were icy, it was in the middle of a snowstorm. She was in labour, he was trying to get her to the hospital. There is no evidence of reckless driving. No proof he did anything wrong. His driving record is exemplary."

"I don't buy it. Why else would he run? He just didn't want to face the music."

Jem's face flushed. She balled her fists and bit her tongue. "Mr. Engles, he left because he was struck with overwhelming grief. Probably guilt too, but not in a legal, avoiding prosecution way. Even if he's not guilty under the law, he still feels that he was responsible. Wouldn't you?"

Bill bounced Emma on his hip. The girl let a spit-bubble fueled laugh go and grasped his lower lip. He peeled her fingers off and kissed her nose. "Cut it out Emma-bear."

Jem glanced at Finn. She'd been so focused on Joe, on helping him and getting his daughter back, she failed to notice how much this man loved his niece. He'd stepped up and taken her in. Raised her to this point all on his own, and by all appearances, he'd done an excellent job of it. He didn't let Emma get lost in the system, or end up in the arms of strangers.

"Look," she softened her tone. "It's obvious how much you love Emma. Try to imagine how Joe would feel about her. She's his daughter. Imagine if someone were to take her from you."

"Isn't that exactly what you're trying to do?"

"Not take her away. Only to let her know her father. You

wouldn't lose her. She'd still be right here in Regina."

He pulled Emma closer and glared at Jem.

"Mr. Engles, she's not yours." Finn took a half-step forward and put a hand on Bill's shoulder. "You've done a wonderful thing, taking care of her. You're a good man, a good uncle. But she's not your child."

"Joe will be returning," Jem said. "You can't adopt her without his consent."

"I won't give her up. I'm her daddy now, not Joe."

Jem set her jaw and exhaled fast through her nose. "I'm sorry you feel that way. I'll be filing to have your temporary custody revoked. All parental rights will be restored to Joe." She pulled out her cell phone and snapped a picture of Emma.

Bill turned away and covered Emma's head with one hand. "Why'd you do that?"

"Joe needs to see his daughter."

Jefferson cleared his throat. "Mr. Engles, you're not going to run are you?"

Bill's shoulders slumped, tears stained his cheeks. "No. Where would I take her? This is her home. She loves the swings."

"Good." Jefferson held out his hand and Bill shifted Emma in his grip and shook it. "Because we'll get an order of protection if we have to."

Bill exhaled, his bravado deflated. "Where the hell has he been anyway?"

"We aren't sure where he was between November and last month." Finn put his hand on Jem's shoulder. "Ms. Stone found him living in the park."

"Living there? Like a homeless guy?"

Jem cleared her throat. "Yes, he's been living on the streets. But he's not homeless, his home is right here. He's just been away."

"Is he in his right mind? I mean who does that, walk away from their life and live on the streets?"

"Lots of people do that." Jem had seen her share of them. But none like Joe. "We think he's suffering from post-traumatic stress disorder. I've arranged for him to see a psychiatrist to work through the trauma of the accident and losing his family. He'll be fine."

"Will he be able to take care of her? To be a good father?"

"I have no doubt."

"Wait." Bill stepped back into the house and emerged a minute later. He handed Jem a picture. "This one's better."

Emma sat on Bill's lap, a fake blue sky in the background. Bill beamed at the camera. Emma laughed and drooled.

Jem smiled. "Thank you."

"Am I going to have to move out?"

Jefferson glanced at Finn. "Why would you have to do that?"

Bill looked at his feet. "It's Joe's house. Joe and my sister, Emma's." He looked at Jem. "They bought it right after they married five years ago. I moved in when he disappeared so Emma'd have a real home. Not my crappy apartment with no yard. If I didn't, they would have foreclosed."

"You've been paying the mortgage?"

"And utilities and everything."

Finn loosened his tie. "Why don't we start with bringing Joe home?"

Jem touched Emma's cheek with her thumb. The baby grabbed her hand and stuck one of Jem's fingers in her mouth. Emma sucked Jem's finger and cooed. Drool dripped down her hand. "She's a happy girl. And Joe is a kind man. He'll be reasonable."

"You don't think I know that? He was always real nice to me. Treated me like a brother. But damn it, he took off and left Emma. I had to bury my sister without him. I've been so angry." He buried his face in Emma's soft hair and his shoulders shook. "I miss her," he whispered. "She never even got to see her beautiful baby girl."

truly wonderful

The next morning, Jem made her rounds through the park. Joe sat cross-legged by the bush. She dropped to the grass in front of him and watched in silence while he ate. When he finished, she filled him in on moving in with Finn. On her fledgling practice.

"Remember, if you need a lawyer, you can count on me. I won't charge you anything."

His eyes narrowed. "Why would I need that?"

Finn's shadow filled the space between them. Joe started and looked up.

Finn extended his hand. "Hi, Joe. I'm Finn."

Joe untucked his legs and scooted backwards, but the branches of the bush prevented his escape. He put one hand on the ground, leaned sideways and brought one foot under his rear end, then pushed himself up.

"Joe, wait." Jem jumped up and blocked his path. She put her hand on his arm. "Look at me. Not at Finn, just me."

He hesitated and cut his gaze to her.

"Do you trust me, Joe?"

He looked from her to Finn and then back to her. One short nod.

"Okay, that's good. We're here to help you. Honest, just to help. Finn too."

He kept his eyes on her, scratched his cheek and ran both hands down the front of his pants. He stole a quick glance at Finn.

"There's no easy way to tell you this." Jem took Joe's hands. "It's something shocking. And wonderful. Truly wonderful." She took a deep breath, her heart in her throat. "Joe, Finn is a police officer."

His hands stiffened and he pulled back. Jem held tight.

"It's okay. It is. The accident wasn't your fault."

He shook his head.

Finn put one hand on Joe's shoulder. "Joe, you couldn't have prevented it. The Regina police shared their investigation with me. You have no legal culpability."

Joe squinted. "Legal?" He turned his head and stared into the distance.

"Joe." Jem touched his cheek. "You did nothing wrong. That road was black ice under fresh snow. You were driving under the limit but it wouldn't have mattered. It was the most unfortunate series of events."

Tears streamed down Joe's face.

"You did everything you could for Emma. But nothing you could have done would have saved her." She glanced at Finn. He nodded. "But Joe, you don't know everything." She pulled a photo out from her jacket pocket and held it out to him. "They saved the baby, Joe. They saved her. You have a daughter."

He spun around and stared at the photo, squeezed his eyes shut and swallowed. When he opened them, he shook his head. His gaze darted around the picture. He inched his arm forward and took it from her, then brought it close to his eyes. He ran his fingers over his daughter's face.

"H-how?"

"Caesarean section."

"But Emma was dead."

"Brain dead." Jem couldn't stop tears from coming. "As soon as they knew they couldn't save her, they put her on a ventilator. Kept her heart pumping long enough to keep oxygen flowing to the baby. Then they delivered your daughter." She rubbed one hand up and down Joe's arm. "In the rush to help her, you got left in the dust. Last thing anyone told you was that Emma died. And then you were gone. You didn't know they were going to do the surgery. The hospital put out a missing persons bulletin. But no one could find you."

He pointed to the photo. "Bill?"

"He's been raising her. In your home. Protecting your house and your daughter. He's done a great job. She's very happy."

His brow furrowed and he cocked his head to one side. "You saw her?"

She looked at Finn. "We both did. Yesterday. She's beautiful, Joe." She smiled. "She has your eyes."

He looked back at the picture. "What's her name?"

"Emma Jean."

He collapsed. Finn caught him before he fell to the ground. Joe buried his face in Finn's shoulder and sobbed, his body quaking. Finn held him in a bear hug and let him cry while a small crowd of park residents gathered behind them.

"Jem?"

She turned to find Angus, his hat gripped in both hands and held to his chest. Frank stood behind him, the crease between his eyebrows deeper than usual.

"Chief all right?"

"He'll be fine, guys, thanks. He's going to go home soon. Home to his daughter."

Tears sprung from Angus's eyes. "That's good." He wiped his

cheek and waved towards Joe. "Good for you, Chief."

Joe released his grip on Finn's jacket sleeve and nodded at Angus, then smiled. He stepped towards Jem and hugged her.

She put her arms around his spare frame and squeezed. The stench of body odor and dirt stung her nostrils but she didn't care. Joe was coming around. And going home.

Jem waited for Joe to relax his grip then looked him in the eye. "Joe, we've made an appointment for you to see a psychiatrist. If he okays it, we're taking you to Regina. I'll file a motion to reinstate your parental rights and revoke Bill's temporary custody. If you've gotten help, some form of professional counseling — that will make things go smoother. Are you ready for all this?"

"Yes. Anything." Joe stood taller, his shoulders back. "I want to see my daughter."

Jem and Finn sat in Thomsons Restaurant in the Hyatt. Jem picked at her eggs Benedict and stared out at the suits rushing down Stephen Avenue Mall.

Almost three hours passed before Sid's call lit up her cell phone. They could come back for Joe.

They arrived at the office with a takeout container. Joe emerged from Sid's office, his face red and eyes swollen. Sid walked behind him with one hand on Joe's shoulder patting in a familiar reassuring gesture Jem had seen him offer Gerald many times.

"Jemima, can I speak to you?" Sid guided Joe to the comfortable leather sofa in the private family room down the hall — the sofa that welcomed the weary and guilt-laden family members of Sid's patients. The sofa that saw tears and angry outbursts from confused and frightened loved ones who wanted to know why their brothers, fathers, mothers, sons were losing their minds and when it would all be better. All be normal. The sofa that bore witness to their utter defeat when the answer was never.

"Of course." She set the take out containers on the marble table in front of the sofa, and handed Joe a plastic fork. "We brought you lunch. Lasagna and salad and iced tea."

"Thank you. I'm starved."

Jem and Finn followed Sid down the hall and into his large office that doubled as a treatment room. She had always appreciated the bright and airy space, the large windows trimmed with white curtains, the tan leather furniture. Sid gave his patients the option of lying on a chaise under the window or sitting in any one of three chairs that dotted the room. He would roll his own chair to whichever spot the patient felt most comfortable.

Gerald always took the chair in the furthest corner from the window. On the rare occasion Jem accompanied him to treatment on Sid's request, she always chose the chaise.

Sid closed the door and sat behind his oversized oak desk. Four years later and nothing had changed, except the patient she'd brought with her. The room still smelled of lemon Pledge and that damn desk pendulum still sat there and dared her to play with it. She pulled back two of the chrome balls and let them drop, like Gerald did every time she came. He would stand next to the desk and lean his elbows on it, his chin in his hands, and watch them tick, tick, tick against one another. Like a countdown announcing the last train to crazy town.

Sid gestured to the two chairs that sat at forty-five-degree angles to his desk. Jem and Finn sat. Finn put one hand over the chrome balls and stopped the ticking pendulum, then took her hand. He didn't need to know the countdown. His feet were firmly planted in sanity-ville.

Sid leaned his elbows on the desk. "Joe's better than I thought. I figured he wouldn't want to talk, but he went on and on with little provocation. I want to see him again, before you take him back to

Saskatchewan. Can you bring him in the morning?"

Jem nodded. "Yes, of course. The more info we have from you the better it will make his application for removal of Bill's temporary custody. Will you provide a formal assessment?"

"I'll draft it this afternoon and finish it up tomorrow morning." Sid tented his fingertips and leaned back in his chair. His signature psychiatrist's pose. "You told him about his daughter?"

Jem squirmed. "Yes, this morning."

"It could have backfired you know."

"I know. But Sid, I had a feeling he'd come around. He'd thrown away everything thinking he'd killed his wife and child. Why wouldn't he try to get it all back if one of them lived?"

"Well it paid off. He told me the whole accident story. As much as he remembers. When the hospital staff talked about his wife and he heard 'dead' he went blank. Wandered away and never went back. He hadn't planned on running away from life, but couldn't turn around. Didn't think he had a reason to." Sid leaned forward. "Did you know that he and his wife met in junior high? In the same school he teaches at now."

Finn blew air from his mouth then pursed his lips. "No wonder he didn't go back. Even work would be a constant reminder."

Sid nodded. "Yes. But less a reminder of his wife, and more of his guilt. It will be a while before he forgives himself. He may never do that. But now he has a reason to go home. To go on. Good job, Jemima." Sid winked. "I think you've saved the man's life."

Jem walked through The Core, the shining mall that anchored downtown Calgary. Finn and Joe flanked her, her arms laced through each of theirs. Most shoppers they passed eyed them with confusion, amusement, or disdain. A god in a silk suit, a down-dressed woman in tank top and capris who could be mistaken for a soccer mom instead of a criminal defense attorney, and a scruffy homeless man with two-day stubble, and torn and filthy clothes who left an acrid stench in his wake.

Let them stare. Nothing mattered today. Nothing except Joe.

"First we'll get you some new clothes and shoes. Then a barber shop. Sound good?" Jem squeezed Joe's arm.

"You don't need to. I can go to the shelter for a shower and a cut. And clothes too."

"Nonsense. You're going home to your daughter. We're going to spiff you up. Make the best first impression on Emma possible."

"I don't know if I can ever repay you."

"No need, Joe." Finn's voice, that sound Jem used to think of as crisp and tight, now resonated like a tenor saxophone playing a heroic ballad. "This is all on us."

Joe tucked his hands in the front pockets of his jeans and looked at his feet. "All right. I'm in your hands." He glanced up at Finn, his cheeks pink. "But no suits. I'm not a shirt-and-tie kind of guy."

Finn laughed. "Understood."

They stopped in men's stores and jeans stores. In Brooks Brothers, Joe settled on leather wing tips and tried on a pair of black boat shoes. Jem turned away when he paced the aisle, staring down at his feet. At least he hadn't chosen a lilac corduroy sport coat. The resemblance to Gerald might have pushed her over the edge.

When they walked out of the shoe store, a young mother sat on a chair feeding an infant. She cooed at the baby and kissed its head. Joe slowed and stared at the child. Tears wetted his cheeks.

By the time they made their way to the barber shop, Joe and Finn were laden with bags. Joe wore a new golf shirt, jeans and sneakers. His old clothes were left at Banana Republic. The sales clerk had picked them up with just two fingers and slid them into a bag, her face contorted in disgust. She tied a knot in the bag and tossed it in a garbage can, then bestowed a steely glare on them.

Joe got a close shave and a haircut, topped off with a head massage that put him to sleep in the chair. Jem sat and waited, her hand held firmly in Finn's, her gaze never leaving Joe's reflection in the mirror. He was serene. At peace. For the first time since she'd met him.

The barber removed the towel from Joe's neck with a snap. Joe woke with a start and jumped out of the chair, his eyes darting around the shop.

Jem went to stand but Finn held her in place. "Let him figure it out."

Joe found Jem's gaze and relaxed. She breathed a deep sigh, and winked at him.

Finn loaded all of the bags into the back of the van and slid the cargo door open. Joe climbed in and Finn slipped into the passenger seat.

"Joe, you've got some options for tonight." Jem glanced in the rear view mirror. Between sandwiches and Oh! Henry's and Joe's new look, he was almost unrecognizable. A thinner version of the picture in the missing person's file.

"I can stay at the shelter."

"Sorry," Finn said. "That's not one of them."

"Why not?"

"Well for one, you no longer look the part." Jem smiled at him in the mirror. "And you'd get rolled for your new shoes."

Joe laughed. It wasn't hesitant or quiet. It was all out.

Finn twisted around in the seat. "We can set you up in a hotel. You could order room service, take a long bath, watch some television."

"That sounds nice."

Finn nodded. "Or you can come back to our place, do all those same things, except we'll cook you dinner."

A small smile crept onto Jem's face. 'Our place.' That had a nice ring to it.

"I don't want to put you out. Not any more than I already have."

"One thing none of this is doing," Jem said, "is putting us out. You pick."

"If it's not too much, I would love to not be alone anymore."

Finn reached back and slapped Joe's knee. "Home it is."

he hates me

Finn carried the bags from their shopping spree into the house and showed Joe to the spare bedroom. He entered the kitchen alone a few minutes later.

Jem was wrist-deep inside a chicken, stuffing whole garlic cloves, quartered onion, and lemon into the cavity. "Where's Joe?"

"He looked exhausted. I suggested he take a shower and a nap."

"Good idea. Dinner will be a couple of hours anyway."

Finn picked up the chef's knife and started cutting carrots into julienne strings. "Do you think he'd let me give him a suitcase? He has nothing to carry his new things home in."

She looked up at him. "I'm sure he'd appreciate that. I know I do." She stood on her tiptoes and kissed his cheek.

"What was that for?"

"For you being about the nicest person I've ever met. And for me being the luckiest woman on earth."

He grinned, his eyes on the carrots and the knife. "Well, gee. Thanks."

"When I get this chicken in the oven, we should make some flight arrangements for tomorrow afternoon."

"And I'm going to call in and take the next couple of days off. This isn't exactly official business."

"I'm glad you're coming." She smashed a garlic clove and tucked it under the chicken skin alongside fresh sage leaves, then rubbed oil on the bird. "If it hadn't been for you, he'd have never learned about Emma. He'd have rotted in that park, alone."

"That's all because of you. Take the credit, Jem. You did this."

"Can I tell you something?" She put the roasting pan into the oven.

"Anything. Anytime."

"I contacted the *Association in Defense of the Wrongly Convicted*. They're like the *Innocence Project*." She tapped the faucet with her wrist and warm water sprung from the chrome.

"I know who they are. I've worked with them in the past, from a police standpoint."

"Of course, sorry. Anyway, I'm going to take on local cases they identify. Pro bono." She dried her hands on a dish towel.

"Sounds perfect. And if you ever need a detective, I know this guy —"

"Yeah, I think I know him too." She took the knife from his hand and set it on the counter, then wrapped her arms around him and stared up at his face. "I love you, Detective Finn Wight."

"And I love you, Jemima Stone, Attorney at Law."

Jem rapped on the spare bedroom door with one knuckle. "Joe? Dinner is ready. Do you want to join us, or sleep some more?"

There was movement inside the room and then the door opened. Joe's short hair was kinked on the right side, his face creased from being smooshed into the pillowcase.

She smiled. "Good nap?"

He rubbed one eye with a balled up fist. "Great."

"You hungry?"

"Starved. It smells wonderful. I'll be right out." He closed the door.

In the kitchen, Finn had set the table for three and decanted a bottle of wine. He glanced up from setting salt and pepper shakers on the table when she entered. "I'm thinking that he should call Bill."

"Tonight?"

"Yeah. Give the guy a heads-up that he's coming home. Better than showing up on the doorstep unannounced."

"I guess. What if he decides to bolt?" Jem picked up a carrot stick and snapped a bite off between her teeth.

"I don't think he will. It's obvious he's got Emma's best interests at heart. But maybe he needs some counseling too."

She nodded. "Hm," she said while she chewed.

"Do you always do formal sit-down dinners?" Joe stood behind Finn, a new golf shirt tucked into crisp khakis, his hair damp and smooth.

"Only for special occasions." Finn patted Joe on the shoulder.

Joe pulled out the chair at the one end of the table and motioned for Jem to sit.

"Why thank you, kind sir. Two gentlemen in the same room. I could get used to this."

Joe smiled. "Better not. I think one is enough, and I can't wait to get home." He sat to her right.

She smiled.

Finn sat at the other end of the table and passed the chicken to Joe. The dishes made their way around and they all filled their plates. They ate in near silence except for polite requests to pass the salt and gravy. Joe piled seconds onto his plate and then drenched a piece of bread in gravy and gobbled that up.

When Finn stood to clear the plates, Joe stood too. "Let me?"

"I'll take the assist any time. How about you clear the food dishes and I'll get dessert. You like apple pie and ice cream?"

"Are you kidding me?" Joe placed dishes next to the sink and sat back down. He wiped a tear from his cheek and stared out the window to the front yard below. "Emma used to bake pie every weekend. Apple was my favourite. She did the crumble topping."

"Well, that's what my favourite bakery does." Finn placed a piece at Joe's elbow and handed one to Jem. Then he topped up everyone's wine and sat with his own piece.

Joe ate every bite.

Finn pushed his pie plate away. "Wow, that was great." He wiped his mouth on a linen napkin and turned to Joe. "We've got flights booked for tomorrow afternoon."

"We?"

Jem patted Joe's hand. "We're coming with you."

Tears welled in his eyes. "Thank you. I can't express my gratitude. For everything you've done."

"Just keep in touch, okay?"

"I promise."

Jem gathered the dessert plates and placed them on the counter next to the sink. She looked at Finn, raised one eyebrow and jerked her head towards Joe.

Finn nodded. "Joe, perhaps you should call Bill tonight. To let him know that you're coming."

"That's going to be hard. I bet he hates me."

"He is angry. Or he has been. But he deserves a heads up after all he's done for Emma."

"Yes. Of course." Joe folded his napkin, then shook it open and folded it again. He looked at Jem. "Will you be on the call too?"

"Sure. We can do it on speaker if you'd like."

His posture relaxed. "Thanks."

With dinner dishes done and another glass of wine under their belts, the three of them sat at the table.

"Ready?" Jem looked at Joe.

"As I'll ever be."

Finn punched Bill's phone number into the wireless handset and pressed the speaker button. After four rings, the phone clicked and then a clattering came through the receiver.

"Hello?" Bill's voice sounded tired. A baby cried in the background.

Tears filled Joe's eyes. He leaned closer to the phone.

Finn cleared his throat. "Mr. Engles, this is Detective Wight and Ms. Stone calling. We have Joe here. Will you speak with him?"

"Joe?" Bill's voice cracked. "Joe, are you really there?"

"Hi Bill. It's me. Is that Emma crying?"

"Yeah. I dropped the phone and woke her up. She's fine."

"She sounds fine. Healthy." Joe put his palms together in front of his face briefly. "I hear you've done a good job taking care of her. I can't thank you enough for that." He wiped his wet cheeks.

"Yeah, we're good."

Jem touched Joe's arm. "Mr. Engles, it's Jem Stone here. We'll be in Regina tomorrow afternoon. I plan to file a motion to have your custody revoked and to revert full parental control of Emma to Joe."

"You don't need to. I'll withdraw it. Just come home, man. We'll be here waiting."

is the honeymoon over?

Sid closed the office door behind Joe, leaving Finn and Jem in the waiting room with their coffees.

Jem sat on the leather sofa, patted the seat next to her and sipped at her to-go cup. Finn settled in beside her and put his arm around her shoulder. She leaned her head against him.

"You done good." He kissed her forehead.

"We done good." She tilted her head up and kissed him, a gentle, lingering touch of lips.

"Man, too bad we weren't somewhere more private." He squeezed her shoulder. "You realize we haven't made love in three days?"

"Uh-oh. Is the honeymoon over?"

"Never." He took her coffee and placed it on the table in front of them, wrapped his arms around her, and dipped his head towards hers.

She ran one hand over his hair then rested it on the back of his neck. They shared a long, slow kiss.

Minutes later, Sid's voice neared the other side of the door. Jem and Finn released their embrace. She ran a hand through her hair to tame it and tugged her shirt down.

Joe and Sid exited the office, Sid in the lead. "He'll see you on Monday." Sid handed Joe a business card. "He's offered ten sessions at no cost. You'll like him. He'll help."

Jem stood. "Who will help?"

Joe handed her the card.

"He's a colleague in Regina. He agreed to counsel Joe."

"Help me through the guilt." Joe stood with his hands in his pockets, his eyes on the ground. "Make sure I don't backslide. But I won't, I know it." He looked Jem in the eye. "Because I have Emma."

Jem returned the card. "Thanks, Sid. I don't know what to say."

"No need to say a thing. Joe," Sid held his hand out. "It's been a real pleasure."

Joe gave Sid's hand a strong shake. "You too, doc. Thanks for everything."

wild-eyed, unshaven and filthy

The cab pulled into the drive and slowed to a stop. Joe stared at his home. He closed his eyes and leaned his head against the back of the seat.

Jem patted his knee.

"It looks the same. Like nothing ever happened. Like Emma will be in there making supper or finishing another painting." He shook his head and pressed the thumb and index finger of one hand into his eyes.

"Tell me when you're ready."

Joe stared a minute longer. "Now. I'm ready now."

Jem and Joe exited the cool air-conditioned back seat and stepped into the waning warmth of a late July evening.

Finn climbed out of the front and turned to the driver. "Pop the trunk?" He pulled out Joe's luggage and set it on the driveway then leaned in the driver's side window. "Can you wait down the drive? We'll be going back to the airport soon."

The cab pulled away and stopped at the entry to the property. Jem, Finn, and Joe stood staring at the house. Jem glanced at Joe. "You okay?"

Tears streamed down his face. "I'm nervous."

Before they could take a step towards the veranda, the door squeaked on its hinges. Bill stood in the entry with Emma balanced on one hip. As soon as he saw Joe, he shut his eyes tight and started to sob. He embraced Emma with both arms. The baby looked from him to Joe, her face screwed up like she was about to cry.

Joe's gaze was fixed on Emma. He seemed unwilling to even blink, his eyes wide, mouth agape.

Bill patted her back and kissed her cheek. "Look Emma, it's your daddy." He pointed at Joe.

Joe squeezed his eyes shut, and began to weep. Emma turned her head away and looked over Bill's shoulder at the open door. He made slow steps down the driveway. "Emma, look." He held one of her hands towards Joe.

Joe touched his fingers to hers. She turned around and looked at him. He sobbed and wiped his eyes with his other hand. "Hello, Emma." He reached up and ran his hand through her hair. She grinned at him but shied away, pulling towards Bill's shoulder.

Bill stood her on the ground. She grabbed him around the leg for support.

Joe laughed. "She can walk already?"

"Not yet. She stands if you hold her up or if she has something to grab. She can pull herself onto the couch and crawl up a few stairs."

Jem dug into her purse, pulled out a small stuffed bear and tapped Joe on the elbow with it. He took it and squatted in front of his daughter.

"Look, sweetheart. Do you like bears? I named this one Jemima." He held the bear out for Emma. She reached out one hand and touched its ear, then grabbed it and hugged it into her face before losing her balance. She landed in the dirt on her diaper-padded bottom.

Joe swooped towards her and picked her up. She squirmed and looked at Bill. Then she stopped and stared at her father's face. She tapped his cheek with one hand, poked his eyelid with one finger. Then she smiled and laughed.

Joe held her close and sobbed. Emma looked confused but she didn't cry, didn't pull away. She grasped his short hair with one fist and pulled. Joe choked on a cry and smiled.

Bill wrapped his arms around Emma from behind, his hands on Joe's shoulders. The two men laughed and wept together.

The sun hung low on the horizon, framing the three of them in orange light. Jem rubbed her hands against her arms and shivered.

Finn took off his coat and placed it over her shoulders. "Maybe we should let them be."

She smiled at him and nodded. "Joe, we're going to head home."

Joe broke away from Bill and stepped towards Jem. "I know I've said this, but I don't know how to repay you. I don't even understand why you cared."

A vision of Gerald, wild-eyed, unshaven, and filthy, running away from her in the park flashed through her mind.

"Something in your eyes. Something told me you were missed."

He hugged her, pressing Emma between them. The little girl squealed with laughter, prompting the adults to laugh along with her.

"You keep in touch, do you hear me? I want regular updates on Emma. Photos and letters and emails, got it?" Jem wiped tears from her cheeks.

"Absolutely."

Jem and Finn walked to the cab. Before sliding into the back seat, she gave Joe and Emma one last wave.

without mothers

Jem leaned on the cool granite of the kitchen island, her face warmed by the morning sunlight. She stared at her grandmother's ring that sat on the counter, the black pearl staring back at her. She poked her index finger into the centre of the platinum disk and pushed the ring around the granite before she picked it up, brought the ring to her ear, and closed her eyes against a wave of sorrow. Gerald was gone for good. The others were finally silent.

She placed the ring into the velvet lining of the leather box she'd bought and snapped the box shut.

She glanced at the pink stationery at her elbow. The page was bare except for the words *Dearest Emma* written in Jem's loose cursive at the top. She slid the page closer, picked up the pen, and tapped it against her cheek. Then she began to write.

We have something in common, little Emma. We are both without mothers. I got to know mine for a while, but I still feel lost at times, no strong woman in my life to help guide me, confide in, share my triumphs and joys, my sorrows and tragedies.

I am sending your daddy a ring that I want you to have when you are old enough. It belonged to my grandmother. She died when I was very young, before I can even remember. I've kept it as a reminder of her, but really, what am I reminded of? Not my own memories, my own feelings. No, it just reminds me that my grandmother is another woman that is not here.

I know your daddy and uncle love you enough to fill the empty space in your life. I will never replace your mother, but I'd like you to be part of my family. I will be here for you, Emma, when you need me. Even when you don't, even just to chat, to connect.

Tell your daddy to send pictures. And visit often. I will come to see you, too. We can play on your lovely swings.

Love to you, sweet girl.

Jemima

kiss her again

The air was crisp but the sun shone bright on a warm Saturday in October. Leaves fluttered in the slight breeze, a rainbow of fall colours surrounded the park. Vibrant reds and oranges and yellows stood out against the background of forest green pine and fir that dotted the riverside.

Jem breathed in the aroma of fall — the cleanliness of pine sap mixed with earthy rotting leaves and just a hint of urine.

She adjusted her fitted woolen jacket and smoothed the front of her ivory skirt. She made her way across the grass, the heels of her new pumps sinking in the soft earth. She shifted her weight and moved along on tiptoes. People on either side of her smiled and nodded.

Frank and Angus stood amid a small crowd of park residents. Had they cut their hair and trimmed their beards? Frank even sported a new hand-me-down coat. They cleaned up pretty nice. Jeremy nibbled on one of her brownies. When she caught his eye, he beamed at her through cocoa covered teeth and waved.

Dean was sandwiched between Anna and Marjorie. Those three were the closest thing Jem had to family, other than the people who called the park home. Beyond them stood a grouping of cops, some in uniform, some in suits, Beryl front and centre, looking pretty in a black dress and red stilettos.

A few feet to her right, Joseph stood strong and proud in a suit and tie. He smiled wide, his cheeks glowed healthy pink. Emma sat on his shoulders in the frilled lilac dress Jem had sent for her. Bill stood beside them, one hand on Emma's back, protecting her to the bitter end.

Fifty feet ahead, Finn stood at attention and watched Jem's approach. A knowing smile graced his face. When she was within two yards, he stepped forward and took one of her hands. He placed his other hand behind her head and bent towards her. One finger lifted the short mesh that hung from her pillbox hat and tickled the tip of her nose. He kissed her right there in front of everyone.

Public displays of affection. Oh how she loved them.

"Kiss her again!"

The crowd broke into laughter. Finn looked around. "If you say so, Angus."

He pulled her to him, put both arms around her and kissed her while their friends cheered.

Someone cleared her throat.

Jem and Finn turned to face a woman who stood in front of the shrub where Joe used to sit. A white judge's robe hung to her calves.

"Normally, kissing the bride waits until after the vows. But Jemima and Finn have made it very clear — we aren't to stand on ceremony today."

about the author

Julie Frayn is the author of *Suicide City, a Love Story*, as well as several short stories, and silly poetry for kids about smashed peas and birds with gastroenteritis.

Praise for Suicide City:

"*Suicide City* is full of dense and deep settings. The It-Feels-Like-You-Are-There type of settings where you imagine you can smell the trash in the dumpster."

"Frayn's writing style is brilliant and her plotting is flawless."

"I was so taken with the characters in Julie's first novel I found myself talking to them - out loud. A master composer of language, Julie's descriptions of place and character are almost tactile."

"Hands down, the best ending line of any book I've read in the thirty-one years I've been a reader. Please, do not miss this exceptional novel!"

Julie can be found all over the world wide web. Please connect with her online:

Twitter: http://twitter.com/juliefrayn
Facebook: http://facebook.com/JulieBirdFrayn
Website: http://juliebird.ca
Amazon: http://amazon.com/author/juliefrayn